D0089470

DEADLY REHEARSAL
". . . murders, classical music and an intellectual appeal."

—*Bellingham Herald* (WA)

ELEGY IN A COUNTRY GRAVEYARD
"With a lovely version of Jane Eyre in the background . . . Peterson skillfully weaves together past and present puzzles. . . . Her protagonist, Jane Winfield, her husband, and her professor, Andrew Quentin, are an amiable and attractive trio."

—*Drood Review of Mystery*

LAMENT FOR CHRISTABEL
"*LAMENT FOR CHRISTABEL* is not a formulaic story, and Ms. Peterson throws in several shocking —yet logical—surprises before the whole thing is over."

—*Rave Reviews*

". . . well-drawn characters . . . and the stunning conclusion leaves one with the feeling of a well-wrought ending to a first-rate mystery."

—*Mystery Newsletter* (Tower Books)

Also by Audrey Peterson

The Nocturne Murder
Death in Wessex
Murder in Burgundy
Deadly Rehearsal
Elegy in a Country Graveyard
Lament for Christabel

Published by POCKET BOOKS

AUDREY PETERSON

A Claire Camden Mystery

DARTMOOR BURIAL

POCKET BOOKS

New York   London   Toronto   Sydney   Tokyo   Singapore

An *Original* publication of POCKET BOOKS

POCKET BOOKS, a division of Simon & Schuster Inc.
1230 Avenue of the Americas, New York, NY 10020

ISBN: 0-671-72970-5

First Pocket Books printing October 1992

10 9 8 7 6 5 4 3 2 1

POCKET and colophon are registered trademarks of
Simon & Schuster Inc.

Cover art by Kye Carbone

Printed in the U.S.A.

*To Win and Jack Wrightson,
delightful guides to
Dartmoor and its lore*

Author's note: Some of the events in the life of Mary Louise Talbot are suggested by those of nineteenth-century novelist M. E. Braddon. For these, I am indebted to Robert Lee Wolff's excellent biography, *Sensational Victorian: The Life and Fiction of Mary Elizabeth Braddon*.

However, the novel *The Specimen* is entirely fictitious and is the invention of the present author.

1

I WAS IN DEVON VISITING BEA CAMDEN, MY EX-MOTHER-IN-law, when the inquest was held on the body of the young woman found on the moor. The town of Morbridge hadn't known that much excitement since Cromwell's army defeated the Royalists in 1646, although the local residents kept an outward cool commensurate with the rural code of stoicism.

Bea had greeted me with a warm hug. "Claire, darling, how lovely to see you!"

As we settled in for our morning coffee, I broached the hot topic of the hour. "Darla Brown was a local girl, wasn't she? Did you know her, Bea?"

"Not really to speak to, although she lived down at the bottom of the road. The mother works in the local factory and the father drives a lorry, so I understand. Darla was the eldest of three. Poor girl—what a dreadful thing!"

"I believe the newspaper said she had been living in London for the past several months. Had she come down here for a visit?"

"Yes. The local word is that Darla was here several

weeks ago for a day or two, then left, and no one in her family has heard from her since. Not that that's as odd as one might think, as she seldom wrote to them in any case."

"I heard on the news that the body was found in a bog out on the moor."

"Yes, she was found by a Dartmoor Letterboxer."

"A *what?*"

"It's a society of dedicated walkers on the moor who find little boxes and mark them with a stamp to prove they found them. I imagine this chap was poking about in the quagmire with his stick, hoping to find a letterbox, and there she was."

"I wonder how long the body had been there?"

"No one seems to know. It appears the police are keeping mum on that score."

I said with a grin, "I may be able to scrounge some information from the horse's mouth."

Bea was gratifyingly curious. "Whatever do you mean?"

"It happens that Neil Padgett, the detective superintendent in charge of the case, is an old acquaintance. When he was posted in London, he knew Miles at the Home Office, and I've seen him since from time to time. Now that he's here in Devon, I've promised to look him up."

"Neil Padgett—I've seen him on the telly when some major crime occurs down here—which isn't all that often, thank heaven."

"Actually, Neil probably won't tell me a thing we couldn't read in the news. By the way, what sort of work did Darla Brown do in London?"

"She was a receptionist in a solicitor's office. She had gained experience in Oliver Bascomb's office here in Morbridge for a time after leaving school, so I expect that's how she qualified."

"I wonder if she went back to her job in London after her visit here?"

"That's one of the mysteries. According to the local grapevine, she called in sick and never turned up again."

"Was she reported missing, do you know?"

"It seems the solicitor himself considered filing a report with the Metropolitan Police, but a young woman in the office said that Darla had hinted about getting married soon. Then they learned she had moved out of her lodgings the week before and decided she must have gone off with the man, married or not."

"Who was the man?"

"No one seems to know. Darla was secretive about the whole business."

Bea bent forward to refill our cups, her salt-and-pepper hair swept back from her handsome face, her large gray eyes studying me. "Well, my dear, enough of grim topics. You're looking very well. How was your flight?"

"Fine. It's good to be back."

"And you'll be on leave until next year?"

"Yes. On sabbatical."

When the semester ended, I had wasted no time winding things up at my university at South Coast in California. I had shipped off two cartons of material for my research project—a biography of a Victorian woman novelist—and after a few drinks with fellow professors in the English department and a farewell party with friends, I was off to London, which had been my second home for the twenty years of my commuter marriage to an English husband who lived in London.

After a day or two settling into my London flat, I had come down to Devon to see my daughter Sally, who was attending the university at Exeter, and at the same time to pay a visit to my former mother-in-law, who was still one of my favorite people.

Bea asked, "Is Sally coming on Saturday?"

"Yes. She'll be driving here in her Mini, of course. It was so good of you to give her the car, Bea."

"A grandmother's prerogative, my dear, and quite selfish, I assure you. I'll see her more often if she can get here easily."

A year ago, when Sally had chosen to go to Exeter, where she followed in the maternal footsteps by making English lit her field of study, she had said, "When you're back in the States, Mums, I'll be close to Beebee"—she still used her childhood name for Bea—"and besides, I love Devon, and I should think Daddy will be pleased."

Actually, her father, who had been at Balliol, no doubt thought that Exeter was rather *infra dig* after Oxford, but I gave him full marks for telling Sally he was happy with her choice.

Bea rarely mentioned Miles to me unless I spoke of her son first. It had been almost two years since the divorce, but while I had pretty much made it through the valley of the shadow, I knew it was still difficult for Bea, although outwardly she and her son were on good terms.

"It's not just the scandal, Claire," she had said over and over at the time. "It's simply *wrong!*"

And I had long since given up trying to defend Miles to his mother.

After lunch, I set off for a walk. Unlatching the gate of the front garden, I looked back at the comfortable old house that had been in Bea's family since the middle of the last century. When the ownership came to Bea, she'd kept it as a summer place, and through the years Miles and Sally and I had spent some great holidays there with his parents. When Miles's father died three years ago, Bea elected to settle in Morbridge, declaring she loved the country and had no wish to go back to London.

As I followed the curve of the road down the hill, a strange-looking lady on a bicycle, her wild gray hair flying, passed me, staring intently into my face as she went by. I had lived in England long enough, off and on, not to be surprised by eccentric characters, so I gave her a little wave and carried on.

Near the bottom of the road I noticed a small cottage that looked unusually shabby for well-kept Morbridge. A few flowers straggled through untended beds, streaked plaster cried out for a fresh coat of paint, and laundry flapped on the lines in the back garden. A sullen-looking boy of eleven or twelve swung by one foot on the sagging front gate.

As I approached, a man in a trenchcoat emerged from the front door of the cottage, saying, "Thank you, Mrs. Brown."

A woman with orange hair followed him out, shouting, "I've had enough of you lot from the police. Don't come back! I'm sick of your questions!"

Trenchcoat shrugged, made his way past the boy at the gate, and walked away.

I watched as the woman who must be Darla Brown's mother slammed the door of the cottage. With a mother like that, I thought, who could blame Darla for escaping to London?

Beyond the cottage, I walked on to the high street, past an ancient alehouse, past the car park with its tourist information office already open to receive the hordes of summer visitors, and over the stone bridge spanning the local stream that alternately rushed or meandered its way to the sea.

The high street was absurdly narrow as it climbed straight up a hillside lined with shops, where cars maneuvered painfully in spaces never intended for their bulk. I picked up a couple of items in the chemist's, dawdled in a bookshop, and came face to face with Stella Bascomb, wife of Oliver, the local solicitor.

"Claire! Bea said you were expected! Have you just come?"

We did the ritual hug. "Yes. I stopped in London overnight to drop off my gear at the flat and came straight down."

Oliver and Stella Bascomb were old Morbridge friends of Bea, whose families had known each other forever, as Bea put it. She and Oliver's father had been friends from childhood, and after his parents died, Bea had become a kind of surrogate mother to Oliver and Stella, who had in turn become courtesy cousins to Miles and me during all the years of our marriage.

Stella Bascomb was one of those women who could look absolutely dazzling or incredibly tacky, but never dull. This was one of her tacky days. Strands of dark hair wandered randomly onto her shoulders and down her back, while the long bones of her face, bare of makeup, made a pale frame for her remarkable eyes.

"I'm desperate for a coffee, Claire. Come along." Stella placed a commanding hand on my arm and led the way to The Singing Kettle— *"Must they come up with these dreadful names?"*—which was comfortably deserted between the lunch hour and tea time.

"So," I began, "how is Oliver?"

"He's an absolute wreck, darling."

"Sticky cases?"

"No, no. It's the Party." Stella's throaty voice moved down a few decibels. "Our M.P. died quite suddenly, and Oliver may be in line to stand for the seat at the by-election."

"How marvelous! Not the death, I mean, but for Oliver."

In a stage whisper, "It would be if it were a sure thing, but there's a hot contest going on behind the scenes." Stella's eyes searched the near-empty tearoom for possible political conspirators. "Incidentally, you're coming to dinner tomorrow evening—did Bea tell you?"

"Not yet. I'm afraid we spent most of our time talking about the murder."

"Oh, God, yes. Poor Oliver. As if he hasn't enough on his plate, the police have been badgering him about the girl. She was his receptionist for a few weeks before she went off to London, you know."

"So I heard. Did you know her, Stella?"

"I remember her vaguely. Sexy little thing, I thought, but rather chubby."

I repressed a smile. To Stella, tall and elegantly bony, anyone with an ounce of flesh was chubby.

"I keep hearing that the body was found on the moor, but *where* on the moor, Stella? Do you know?"

Stella's enormous dark eyes looked straight into mine; then her glance swooped down to the table. Picking up the salt cellar, she examined it with the concentrated interest one would give to a rare object in a museum.

"The body?" she said vaguely. "Oh, yes, it was off the Downs Road."

"Near your place?"

"No, no. Beyond the tor. The location was marked

on a map in the local newspaper, much to the irritation of the police, I gather, as it encouraged onlookers to engage in morbid curiosity."

"I'm curious myself, Stella, though not really morbidly. I'd like very much to see the place. Can you show me where it is?"

Stella shrugged. "I expect so, if you're sure you want to go."

Five minutes later we drove out of Morbridge in Stella's aging Jaguar and headed for the Downs Road. I didn't tell Stella my reason for wanting to see the scene of the crime, but I knew I'd be seeing Neil Padgett, who was in charge of the case, and I wanted to have a little background for intelligent discussion when we met.

8

2

THE TOWN OF MORBRIDGE LIES ON THE EASTERN SIDE OF the moor, not far from the boundary of Dartmoor National Park, and a few miles from High Tor, one of the many granite outcroppings that dot the tops of ridges all over the moor.

Stella Bascomb drove out of the town onto a road that rose sharply, passing a spate of bed-and-breakfasts and one very upscale hotel, standing in manicured grounds, reminders that tourism was a major industry in this part of the country. As we climbed, the road narrowed to a twisting tunnel between vertical banks of hedgerows or stone walls, where oncoming cars either waited at the occasional wider spot for us to pass or came straight on, leaving it to Stella to do the squeezing.

After a mile or so of this, we emerged into open vistas of cultivated farmland adjacent to the road, beyond which rose the barren downs of the moorland. On a wooded slope on our left, as we flashed by, I glimpsed the roof and chimneys of Herons, the

9

Bascomb place, the house hidden from view by a high wall and screening trees.

Presently the car rattled across a cattle grid, and now the green fields were gone and we saw only the rocky soil of the moor, where black-faced sheep roamed freely, grazing on the stubby growth of gorse and heather. The barren and desolate landscape exerted its special brand of magnetism, haunting the senses. On our right as we approached the summit, we could see the immense boulders of High Tor along the crest of the down. A few hikers, perhaps lured out by the warm sun, made slow-moving dots along the hill as we passed.

Beyond the tor, the road wound on through the rolling downs, where now and then some moorland ponies looked at us with patient, incurious eyes as we passed, their shaggy brown bodies shuffling among the gorse bushes.

The sun that had blazed with unaccustomed warmth for the last few days slid abruptly behind some nasty-looking clouds, and within minutes we saw drops of rain on the windscreen.

"Damn! There goes our sunshine." Stella glanced over at me. "Will you be all right?"

"Sure." I pulled a plastic rain hat from the pocket of my windcheater.

A mile or so further on, Stella drove slowly, peering to her left. At sight of a road, she said, "It must be here somewhere—let's try this one," and turned onto what was little more than a rough track. At first there was nothing, but a turn in the road revealed a hollow where we saw several parked cars and some men bent low to the ground, searching. A large pond, dotted with tufts of grass, was ringed with stakes, to which the familiar police tape was attached.

Bits of clear sky were visible on the far horizon, but

the unremitting darkness overhead made it seem more like dusk than afternoon. While the rain was still only a misty drizzle, a sharp wind had come up, biting through my light jacket as I stepped out of the car.

Stella, undeterred by the presence of the police, walked to the edge of the tape and pointed to the pond. "It must be just there, you see."

A car door slammed behind us and I turned to see Detective Superintendent Neil Padgett himself coming toward us.

"Claire!" He held out both hands to mine. "It's very good to see you. How long have you been in Devon?"

"I came in this morning. I'm staying with Bea."

I made the introductions, not missing Stella's scrutiny of my face. One of the problems with divorce was the incurable matchmaking of friends. I was pleased to see Neil Padgett—an intelligent, pleasant man, whose company I enjoyed—but I was not prepared to make more of it than that.

A uniformed officer approached Neil. "Good afternoon, superintendent."

"Any luck, sergeant?"

"Afraid not, sir. A few bits and pieces have turned up, that's all."

Neil turned to us. "The scene-of-crime chaps are making a final check."

I said, "Neil, I'm sure I shouldn't ask this, but do you know as yet the cause of death?"

A pause. "Actually, it's no secret now, as it will be disclosed at the inquest tomorrow morning. The report says she was poisoned."

Neil went off to make a circuit of the men at work, speaking briefly to each one, while Stella and I stood gazing at the pool where someone had dumped Darla Brown's body, to be sucked down into the sticky mud.

Poisoned? That was a surprise. I had guessed it to be

a crime of physical violence: strangling, most likely, or a throat-cutting, Jack-the-Ripper killing. So much for the passing stranger. Poison suggested someone who knew her, someone who planned to kill her—and of course, someone who knew the moor well enough to find this place to dispose of her body. Someone who knew this was not a mere pool of water but a mire, with its sinister tentacles ready to hold the body down and out of sight. Now, the warm days of late spring had lowered the level of the water enough to make the body visible.

We saw Neil and one of the officers step onto a patch of turf that provided a foothold of solid ground, surrounded by the turgid waters of the mire. They both gazed downward, the officer probing with a long stick, then raising it to reveal the clinging mud at its end, and pointing to a line that indicated the depth of the water. Both men nodded.

I shivered as the wind whipped the folds of my jacket. Abruptly, fat drops of rain gathered together into a solid sheet of water, and Stella and I ran for the car. We saw Neil step back to the edge of the pool, speak briefly again with the sergeant, and walk toward my side of the car.

I rolled down the car window for Neil, who asked, "Are you coming to the inquest tomorrow?"

Stella answered for me. "Absolutely. We wouldn't miss it!"

"Good. Well, then, I can manage lunch afterward. Would you care to come along—both of you?"

Stella didn't hesitate. "It's most kind of you, but I'm afraid I'm booked. Claire, you're free, are you not?"

Why not? I thought. "Yes, I'd like that very much, thanks."

"Tomorrow, then."

Turning the car, Stella followed the cart track until we reached the road to Morbridge. As the towering granite shapes of High Tor came into view, she glanced over at me. "He's a most attractive man, Claire, and he does seem smitten."

"Stella, honestly. How do you know he isn't married with half a dozen children?"

"Oh, dear—is he?"

"Well, no. As I understand it, he and his wife live apart."

"There, you see—"

"Stella, you're as bad as Bea."

Ever since the divorce, my mother-in-law's dearest wish, once she had given up hope Miles and I would get back together, was to see me cozily settled into matrimony with some worthy creature. I couldn't convince her that was the last thing I needed. What with teaching, my all-consuming work on my research project, and keeping tabs on Sally, my life was satisfying enough. A few congenial friends made great social companions without complications. Ay, there was the rub, and I knew it. I enjoyed men as friends, but emotional involvement? Forget it.

It was no good saying all this to Stella. I was sure she couldn't imagine life without Oliver and took it for granted that marriage was equally indispensable for everyone else.

But hadn't I once felt that way myself? In the early years with Miles, when the world—as dear old Matthew Arnold said—seemed to lie before us like a land of dreams, so various, so beautiful, so new, hadn't I in fact enthusiastically sought mates for my divorcing friends, not knowing that I would one day find myself on that darkling plain? Arnold had warned that there were no certitudes in life, but who listens to a Victorian poet these days?

3

THE INQUEST INTO THE DEATH OF DARLA BROWN WAS HELD in the town hall in Kings Abbey, a market town some miles to the south of Morbridge. Bea came along with Stella and me, declaring she wouldn't miss it for worlds, especially as I knew the detective superintendent in charge of the case.

As we took our seats, the small room began to fill, and I saw Bea and Stella nod to acquaintances from Morbridge who may have known Darla or who were just plain curious.

The members of the jury took their places, and the coroner, a middle-aged man with thinning hair, called his first witness, the young man who had found the body on the moor. In his early twenties, I guessed. A pleasant face.

"Your name, please, sir."

"William Trask."

"Your address?"

"The Raven, Rose Lane, Morbridge."

"Thank you. Now, will you please describe the events of Sunday last, pertaining to this enquiry?"

"Yes, sir. I set off with my dog to go letterboxing."

"Excuse me, sir, will you explain the term 'letterboxing' for those who may not know it?"

"Yes, of course." The eager look of the enthusiast lit the face of William Trask. "Many of us who enjoy walking on the moor are members of the Dartmoor Letterbox Society. To put it simply, we place a watertight container of some sort at a location on the moor—under a rock or in a natural hole in the turf, for example, taking care not to disturb the natural environment. We then record clues to its location according to the ordinance survey map. All the boxes are listed in our catalogue, and our challenge is to locate as many as we can."

"Thank you. Please go on."

"Well, then, on Sunday last, I had reached the location where I found a new letterbox. I had stamped the visitor's book in the box and taken the stamp from the box to mark my own collection, when my dog began tugging at his lead. Seeing no sheep nearby, I let him go, and he led me to the edge of a bog, barking wildly.

"As we got nearer, I became aware of a dreadful stench. Something was floating in the water, some sort of fabric. Then I saw strands of hair, and when I reached the edge of the pool, I looked down through the water and saw it was the body of a woman, half-buried in the mud."

"Can you describe the face of the person you saw?"

William Trask looked stricken. "It was quite dreadful. The face was horribly swollen, and sort of greenish-black, and the tongue was protruding. I only thought it was a woman because of the long hair and

15

the clothing, which looked like the remnants of a blouse and skirt."

The witness stopped, taking a deep breath, and the coroner waited patiently before going on.

"And what did you do then?"

"I fastened the dog's lead and hurried back to my car. Then I drove to the police station in Morbridge to report what I had found."

"Thank you, Mr. Trask. That will be all."

The police constable from the Morbridge station was called next and described following William Trask to the site, confirming his story, and calling from the patrol car to notify the senior divisional officer—Detective Superintendent Padgett—of the finding of the body.

The next witness was the victim's mother, the orange-haired woman I had glimpsed at the door of the cottage, hurling angry words at the police officer. No anger now. Wearing a black skirt and dark blue jacket—her best effort at mourning, evidently—she walked slowly to the witness chair and sat down, clutching a leather handbag against her chest. Her face was heavily made up in a now outmoded fashion: the powder base, slightly darker than her own pale skin, covering the face and chin but leaving a line on the neck where it stopped. Brows penciled in, mascara thick on the tips of the lashes, eyeliner cruelly emphasizing the wrinkles of nature around the eyes, lipstick a shade too bright.

The coroner began gently. "You are Mrs. Leola Brown, of number seventeen, Abbey Road, Morbridge?"

Nervously, through tight lips, she spoke in a hoarse whisper. "Yes, sir."

"We shall not keep you long, Mrs. Brown. We should like for you to tell us how you came to believe the body of the young woman just described to us was that of your daughter, Darla Brown."

"It was on the telly. They was asking for anyone to come forward if anything shown was familiar. There was pictures of parts of a blouse and skirt like one of Darla's. Red stripes, it had. You couldn't tell it was red still, after being in the water and all, but the sleeves had a cuff with a bit of lace that looked like what she wore last time she was home for a visit."

"And when was that, Mrs. Brown?"

"It's been a month and more."

"Thank you. Was there any further indication of identity?"

"Yes. It was the gold locket. Well, not proper gold, but it was expensive all the same, she told us."

"Can you describe this locket, please?"

"Yes, sir. It was shaped like two hearts, one beside the other but overlapping like, and there was a letter 'D' on each one."

The coroner nodded to the clerk, who opened a flat box, lifted out a tarnished chain with a darkish object suspended from it, and offered it to the witness.

"Is this the object you described?"

As she took the locket in her hand, the woman's face, held so stiffly till now, began to waver.

"Yes, that's the one." She groped in her handbag, finding a tissue with which to dab at her eyes.

The coroner moved quickly on. "Do you know when and how your daughter acquired this locket?"

Mrs. Brown blew her nose and sniffled. "She had it before she went off to London, of that I'm sure. She said a gentleman friend gave it to her, but she never said who he was."

"Was there any significance in the use of two initials rather than the usual one?"

A flicker of pride and a half-smile. "She said the 'D'

was for Darla, of course, and it meant 'double love.' Like one 'D' was for love, two was double."

"I see. I have no further questions." The coroner thanked the witness and extended the sympathy of the court in her loss.

Looking relieved, Leola Brown went back to her seat in the front row between a red-faced, beefy man and a thin girl of perhaps fourteen, with pale freckled skin and red hair, its color no doubt the original shade that her mother now tried to match in her own hair with tints.

The next witness was the beefy man.

"Your name, please?"

"Floyd Brown."

"You are the husband of Mrs. Leola Brown, who has just testified before us?"

"Yes, sir."

"And you live at the same address?"

"That's right."

"You are the father of Darla Brown?"

"In a manner of speaking, yes. That is, I'm her stepfather, but the missus and I was married when Darla was a little mite—three or four years old—so I've been like a father to her." The man looked oozily smug to me, but I could have been wrong.

"The young lady was known as Darla Brown. Was she then legally adopted?"

"No, sir. It didn't seem as if that was needed. She was always a part of the family, like, and used the name same as the others."

"Thank you. Now, Mr. Brown, I believe you were taken to the mortuary to assist in identifying the body of the young woman found on the moor?"

"Yes, sir. The officer warned us it was a pretty grisly sight and asked if we'd rather I'd go instead of the wife, so I did."

"Were you able to make a positive identification?"

"Not at first, sir." His red face grimaced, and he rubbed his forehead with the back of his hand. "I couldn't be sure of the face, as it was swollen up and sort of fallen away in places. The long fair hair could have been hers all right." The man stopped and stared at the floor.

"Was there any further means of identification?"

The man frowned. "Yes, sir."

The coroner waited, but Brown seemed to be stuck again.

"Can you tell us what this was?"

Brown squirmed in his chair, crossing and uncrossing his legs. "Well, sir, the doctor asked if she had any scars and that."

"And did she?"

"Yes, sir, there was one as I knew of."

"Will you describe this, please?"

"Yes, sir. It was a whitish scar, about an inch long, sort of raised up."

"Like a welt?"

"Right."

"And where was this mark?"

Another pause. "It was just here." Floyd Brown pointed to a spot on his own abdomen.

The coroner spoke to the clerk. "Let the record show the witness is pointing to a location between the hip bone and the pubic area."

"Do you know the origin of this scar?"

"Yes, sir. She accidentally cut herself when she was getting ready to shave her legs."

"And how long ago was that, Mr. Brown?"

"Oh, a year ago or thereabouts."

"You had seen this scar before?"

Now Brown looked directly at the coroner. "Well, sir, I was at home when the accident happened. Darla was in her dressing gown and ready to step into the bath, when she called out to me to bring her a plaster. Blood was pouring out, so I opened the bandage for her, and of course I could see where the cut was, before I left the room."

"Have you anything further to add, Mr. Brown?"

"No, sir."

"Then you may step down. Thank you."

Looking relieved, Brown resumed his seat beside his wife, and was followed by the local dentist from Morbridge, who made the final confirmation of Darla's identity from his records.

"Miss Darla Brown made only one visit to my office, two years ago in March, complaining of severe toothache. I took full-mouth X-rays and found the need for considerable work to be done, but she would consent to only one filling, where a tooth was dangerously decayed. As for the painful tooth, I suggested it might be saved through a root canal procedure, but the young lady rejected that course as too expensive, and requested that I extract the tooth, which I did."

The coroner asked, "You examined the body in question at the mortuary, sir?"

"Yes. No further dental work had been done, and the identification was perfectly clear. The locations of the silver filling and the extraction performed by me were identical to those on the body I examined."

Now it was the turn of the Home Office forensic pathologist, a man of considerable reputation who served over a large area of southwestern England.

"I believe you were present at the place where the body was found, sir, before it was removed?"

"Yes, I was called to the scene by the officer in charge of the investigation."

"And you performed the postmortem examination of the body in question, sir?"

"Yes, at the mortuary at the Royal Devon and Exeter Hospital at Wonford."

After describing the height, weight, and approximate age of the deceased, the doctor gave the opinion that the death had occurred approximately four weeks earlier and that the deceased had probably been placed in the water of the bog not long after death, but certainly not before.

The coroner asked, "There was no evidence of drowning, then?"

"None whatever. To continue, when the womb was examined, it revealed a fetus of approximately nine to ten weeks' maturity."

There was a stir in the courtroom. I glanced quickly at Darla's mother but saw no sign of surprise. Evidently Neil or one of his officers had prepared her for this bit of news.

The coroner went on. "What can you tell us, sir, of the cause of death?"

"The body showed no signs of physical violence. No injuries to the skull, no indication of strangulation, nor of stabbing or knife wounds. I then checked for needle-marks and found no evidence of habitual use of injected illegal substances. However, when the viscera was opened, I was certain I detected the odor of cyanide."

The doctor laid his notes in his lap and leaned back in his chair. As a university lecturer myself, I recognized the sure sign that he was about to make a point that might be an aside but was of particular interest.

"It's a curious thing," he said, "that contrary to the popular belief that observers always note the odor of bitter almonds associated with the ingestion of cyanide, in actual fact, only about thirty to forty percent of persons, whether doctors or laymen, are able to detect this odor. It is merely a gratuitous fact, an accident of olfactory genetics, no doubt, that I am one of that minority of persons. However, even if the pathologist in a given instance does not detect the odor, it is likely that among the many persons present —the assistants, the police, and so forth—someone will do so, as the odor is extremely pronounced.

"In the present instance, I recommended to the laboratory that in addition to the usual tests, they should examine the stomach contents for the presence of cyanide in the body in question, and the result was positive."

"Your conclusion?"

"The victim's death occurred as a result of cyanide poisoning."

Again, there was a murmur among the spectators, as the doctor stepped down and Detective Superintendent Neil Padgett was called.

I noted with interest what a fine presence Neil made as he took the witness chair. Solid body, dark hair still thick although he must be in his late forties, serious brown eyes, pleasant mouth, an air of natural command tempered with modesty—trustworthy, intelligent, and he had all the qualities that must have combined to advance his career to his present position. I could feel Bea beside me, bursting with approval.

In answer to the coroner's questions, Neil described the procedures that followed the finding of Darla Brown's body and stated that an intensive investigation was under way to find the person guilty of this heinous crime, although no suspect was at present in custody.

The inevitable verdict of "Murder by person or persons unknown" was delivered by the coroner, and the hearing was adjourned until further evidence should be forthcoming.

As we made our way out of the hall, Bea pressed my arm. "I quite like your Mr. Padgett, Claire."

When I had told her of Neil's invitation to lunch after the inquest, and asked her to come along, she had reacted as I thought she would. "Claire! Of course I'll not come. You two go along. Stella and I have all sorts of shopping to do!"

Bea was a darling and I loved her dearly, but even if Neil asked me, I thought, I couldn't marry him just to make her happy.

4

My lunch with Neil Padgett was as pleasant as I expected. Good Italian food, over which we managed to dispose of a bottle of my favorite Orvieto Classico.

I asked how he liked life in Devon.

"Less hectic than London. More administrative work than I'd choose, but it was a step up for me, as you know. My boy is at school near Torquay. I pop over to see him now and then."

We talked children for a while. Then Neil said, "And what's new with M. L. Talbot?"

I groaned. "I've done only one more chapter of the biography since I saw you at Christmas. It's impossible to get on with the writing while I'm teaching a full program."

Mary Louise Talbot, the subject of my long-term research, was a Victorian novelist who began publishing as "M. L. Talbot" to disguise the fact she was a woman. A popular bestseller in her day, she had faded from view as literary fashions changed in the twentieth century. I was writing her biography, partly be-

DARTMOOR BURIAL

cause no one else had done it, and moreover because,
dated or not, I thought her life and her work had
something to say about the status of women, both then
and now.

The first time I met Neil, I was pleased to find
someone who had not only heard Talbot's name but
had actually read some of her novels. In fact, it was
the only thing I did remember about him for some
time. We met at one of those London parties Miles
and I had so much enjoyed together in the past—a
mix of artists and theater people, with some of Miles's
cohorts from the Home Office and a Member of
Parliament or two thrown in for good measure.

That evening, I had already begun to know our
marriage was in trouble but I didn't know why. Miles
was as full of charm as ever, but his eyes slipped over
me and away, darting into distant corners of the room.

Another woman? I watched and saw no obvious
candidate, hating myself for my suspicion. Neil
Padgett came as an absorbing distraction, quickly
forgotten in the weeks of disaster that followed.

After the divorce, we agreed that I should keep the
flat in Bedford Square, adjacent to the British Museum. When I came back to England last summer, I ran
into Neil in the British Library and asked him to the
flat for a drink with some friends who were dropping
by. We had a couple of evenings at the theater after
that, Neil saying at first that his wife was out of town,
then on the last occasion admitting they were separated and that he was slated to take a new post in
Devon the following month.

Neil and I met again when I flew over to London to
spend Christmas with Sally. He had come up to the
city on a case and we met for lunch, but he was called
away before we had finished our coffee and I didn't see
him again. Since then, we had exchanged a few

25

postcards. Knowing Bea lived in Morbridge, he asked me to give him a ring when I came down to Devon, and I gave him the news of my upcoming sabbatical. Not exactly the hot romance envisioned by Bea and Stella, but a friendship I enjoyed.

At our lunch after the inquest, our talk inevitably turned to the murder.

I said, "I was surprised to learn about the cyanide. It must be difficult to get hold of it."

"Yes. It's not as widely used as one supposes. And of course, it's sold under all sorts of restrictions. It's used in some industries, and also by farmers, to dispose of rabbits or moles that are causing problems. We're checking all possible sources in a wide area, but it may not have been purchased recently. People could have the stuff sitting about for months or years."

"Yes, I see. By the way, I noticed that Darla's mother didn't seem surprised by the news of the pregnancy. Had she been told?"

"Yes. We hoped she would know who the father was, but no luck."

"Did anyone ask the sister?"

"The freckle-faced child? Mmm. Might be worth a try."

"I can see why Darla might not want to confide in her mother. Not an endearing lady, in spite of her sniffles at the inquest." And I described Mrs. Brown's shouting at the police officer as I passed the cottage.

Neil smiled. "Yes, I heard about that. Our chap got the impression the mother was furious when Darla went off to London. There was rather a dustup over it, but of course she didn't say what it was about."

"Maybe Darla was contributing to the family finances while she was working and still living at home."

"Yes, very likely. We're having surprising difficulty

getting any useful information about the girl. We sent a man up to London and didn't get much. No one in the house where she lodged seemed to know anything about her. The only morsel he gleaned, as everyone in Morbridge seems to know, was from the young lady in the solicitor's office where Darla was employed, who reported Darla had planned to be married soon. But no one knows who's the lucky swain."

"I do find that surprising. In my experience, girls usually chatter on about their boyfriends. My students certainly do, and so does my daughter."

"Exactly. We're still looking up everyone we can find who talked with Darla on her last visits to Devon. It seems she was in Morbridge not only last month but also two months or so earlier, in February. Nothing useful as yet."

Over our coffee, Neil asked how long I was staying in Devon.

"Just through the weekend. Then I must get back to London and settle into some serious work."

"Dinner some evening?"

"Yes, I'd like that. Bea has booked us for tomorrow, but Sunday evening is free."

"Good. Let's say Sunday, then? By the bye, I've established the Incident Room here in Kings Abbey. If you hear any local gossip, do let us know."

Back at Bea's place, my jet lag and the wine at lunch caught up with me, and I slept soundly for a couple of hours. Waking, I remembered Bea was expecting someone for tea and did a quick freshening up before staggering down the stairs.

In the drawing room, Bea said, "Claire, dear, you remember my friend Mabel Thorne?"

"Yes, of course."

Mabel lived in the third house down the road, as I

recalled. A tall, imposing woman without a trace of warmth, not at all the sort of person one would expect as Bea's friend, but the two women were members of the same church congregation, and by village standards that was bond enough, I supposed. Not that Morbridge was actually a village—more properly a small town—but the principle was the same.

"Good afternoon, Mrs. Camden." No first names for Mrs. Thorne, I noted, as I returned her greeting. Understandable, certainly, for a lady in what I guessed was her seventies. The informalities of today would only make her uncomfortable.

Now I saw that the woman I remembered as ponderously stout had shrunk, the bones in her neck and arms, once covered with flesh, poking sharply through the black fabric of her dress, her face elongated as the skin sagged where once there had been a ring of fat. I noticed a cane on the floor beside her chair, where she sat sternly upright.

"A touch of rheumatism," she said, gesturing impatiently toward the cane. "Such a bother."

More than a touch, I thought, but said nothing.

Bea handed me my tea and refilled Mabel's cup, saying, "I expect the warm weather helps a bit, my dear?"

Dismissing the subject of her ailments, Mabel said abruptly, "I had a visit from a policeman yesterday. He wanted to know if Harriet had written any news of Darla Brown, and I said she had not."

I remembered that her granddaughter Harriet, after living in Morbridge for some years with her grandmother, had gone to work in London six months or so ago.

Bea said, "She must have seen something of Darla in London, did she not?"

"In the beginning, yes, they seem to have met once

or twice, but she has not mentioned Darla for a very long time. The policeman pressed me rather unduly, I thought. He insisted that surely two young women from the same town in the country would see each other often in the city. I said, not at all. They were at school together, but they were never close, even here in Morbridge."

I asked, "What was Darla like, Mrs. Thorne?"

A lifted eyebrow and a fractional pause. "She was not at all Harriet's sort of person. A flighty girl, I should have said. When they were still at school, Darla would sometimes come to help Harriet with her maths. She was clever enough, I daresay, but from the fragments I heard of her conversation, she seemed chiefly obsessed with boys. There were sly laughs and innuendos coupled with various boys' names. I expect it made Harriet uncomfortable, as she was not yet interested in the opposite sex."

Translated, I thought, this meant boys were not yet interested in Harriet. How well I remembered my high school days in California when girls who were already dating used to torture those of us who hadn't been asked out yet with lurid hints of sexual adventure.

Bea smiled. "And did your policeman accept your word and go away?"

"Not altogether. He asked for Harriet's address in London."

"The police are very thorough, I believe, especially in a case of murder."

"Yes, I expect so." A look of indecision crossed Mabel's face. Then she seemed to make up her mind. "You see, it's awkward, as in Harriet's last letter to me she said she was taking a new post and leaving her residence—what I believe is known as a 'bedsitter.' She wrote that she would give me her new address when she had settled in, but I have not had another letter from her since that time."

Bea frowned. "But Mabel, when was that?"

"It was three weeks ago."

"How odd! Doesn't she write to you every week?"

"Yes, normally. But of course, young people can be busy with their own lives. The move must have been a sudden decision, as she said nothing of it when she was here at the Easter holidays." The back stiffened another fraction. If Mabel Thorne was hurt by Harriet's neglect, she had no wish to show it.

Then, with quick resolve, she said to me, "Mrs. Camden, when you return to London, I wonder if you would be kind enough to call at Harriet's last lodgings? It's quite impossible for me to go, as you can see. Someone there might know her whereabouts."

I could only guess at the effort it cost this proud woman to ask for help, and I assured her I'd be happy to see what I could find out about her granddaughter.

"How very kind of you. If you would care to call on me, I shall give you the address."

Bea tactfully shifted the talk to the upcoming church sale, saying, "Claire brought some lovely things for the jumble. Let me show you."

Mabel ran a sharp eye over my items of cast-off clothing, an old lace tablecloth I'd always hated, and a set of glassware I never used. She nodded with stiff approval. "These will bring a good price, I should think."

The two ladies debated some of the knottier questions of protocol among the members of the Women's Institute. One elderly lady had "always" helped with the pricing but was now "failing" and must be given another task without being offended. The young mother who brought her obstreperous toddler must either keep him subdued or be given the sweets stall, where presumably the infant could be controlled with lollipops.

When Mabel had gone, I asked, "How long has Harriet lived with her grandmother?"

"Since she was eight or nine, I believe. Her father was Mabel's only child, and when he was killed in an accident, she took Harriet to live with her."

"And the mother?"

"Mabel has never mentioned her daughter-in-law, but the town gossip has it that she had run off a year or so before her husband's death, leaving Harriet with him."

"Were they living here in Morbridge?"

"No. In a suburb of London, as I recall."

"Mabel's looking very ill. She seems to have lost a lot of weight."

"Yes. It's been a gradual but steady loss. She must be in pain, but she refuses to give way to it, as you see."

Remembering Neil's desire to talk with anyone who knew Darla, I said, "Perhaps the police could track Harriet down."

Bea shook her head. "I'm sure Mabel would rather not ask for their help just yet."

"But Bea, what if something's happened to the girl?"

"Then someone in London would surely report her missing, would they not?"

We looked at each other for a long moment.

Then I said what was in both our minds. "No one reported Darla Brown missing, did they?"

5

THE NEXT MORNING I SLEPT LATE, STILL A VICTIM OF THE eight-hour time difference from California. No matter how often I made the flight, my biological clock took four or five days to believe that night was day.

Bea had gone to a church meeting, and I was still in my robe in the kitchen, finishing breakfast, when Sally arrived, bubbling with news.

"Mums, you'll never guess! Remember I wrote about Jason, in my tutorial group? He lives here in Morbridge?"

"Vaguely."

"Well, he's Jason *Trask!*"

"Yes?"

"Oh, Mums—you told me on the phone you and Beebee went to the inquest on Darla Brown."

"Yes, we did. Oh, I see—you mean Trask, the young man who found the body?"

"Exactly! He's Jason's *brother!* Jason came to see me this morning, asking for a ride into Morbridge. He knew Darla fairly well, it seems, and the police want to talk to him about her. Also, he often goes letterboxing with his brother and he's promised to show me the place where William found her!"

"Well, darling, I suppose I should go tut-tut and say what morbid curiosity, but the fact is, Stella Bascomb took me out there yesterday."

Sally giggled. "Good old Mums. By the way, Jason's dying to meet you. He's actually read some of la Talbot's novels and he's thrilled that you're writing her life."

We heard footsteps in the passage, and Bea came in, face glowing from her walk in the fresh morning air.

"Sally!"

I watched in amusement while they hugged and exclaimed. People who said Sally resembled me had never met Bea and seen the source for Sally's striking gray eyes, now mirroring those of her grandmother.

I poured coffee for both of them while Sally gave us the latest scoop on her lecturers—the ones she liked and those she didn't—her current reading, her friends, and her dates, coming back to Jason Trask to fill Bea in on the great news of his connection with the murder.

"He talked about Darla as we drove in today. He tried to sound cool, but I think he had a crush on her. You can always tell."

"By the way, darling, Stella Bascomb's invited Bea and me to dinner tonight. Shall I ask if you can come?"

"Oh, thanks, no. It sounds too grim, and besides, Jason wants me to go to a dance club with some friends."

Bea smiled. "Probably just as well, then. Stella's having her local lady to serve, so it must be one of her proper affairs. An extra person would no doubt upset her table."

When Bea and I arrived at Herons that evening, Stella Bascomb was transformed from the pale, unkempt creature of the day before into a stunning queen of the night, her black hair swept into a coil, her cosmetics artfully applied to give a glow to her olive skin and enhance her startling black eyes. In her long wool skirt and knit top, expensively casual, with silver earrings and bracelet her only ornaments, she looked fully prepared to take on the job of wife of a Tory Member of Parliament.

Making a passing introduction or two, she gave us our sherry and left us to mingle with the guests. Presently, Oliver, who had been in deep conversation as we arrived, swooped down upon us, greeting Bea and clasping me in his arms.

"Claire, darling! Beautiful as ever!"

"Hello, Oliver."

I had to fight to overcome my irrational distrust of men as handsome as Oliver. He really did seem pleased to see me. His smile was warm, his eyes clear. Why did I find his charm so resistible? It wasn't his fault if he assumed all women must quiver at his touch—probably most of them did.

After the usual exchange of news, Oliver moved on, and I found myself chatting with a doctor from Exeter and a white-haired man who didn't hear a word we said but smiled benignly at us.

The doctor rolled her eyes. "Can't persuade him to get a deaf aid."

At dinner, I saw the table was set for ten and Stella had managed an even number of men and women. Good thing I hadn't brought Sally. The deaf gentleman sat at Stella's right and the doctor at the opposite end at Oliver's right. I suspected that some of the guests were friends who had some influence in party politics, although nothing so crass was openly discussed.

As the courses came and went, the conversation ranged over sundry topics from the weather to the prospects for Wimbledon. To entertain me as a visitor, someone asked if I'd heard any of the Dartmoor legends, setting off a lively competition around the table to cap each story with one more bizarre.

Oliver began with the story of the Old Birch Tor Mine, which was said to have seams of gold, but when anyone tried to climb down the shaft, an old raven croaked a warning and a ghostly hand holding a knife cut through the climber's rope, sending him to an untimely death.

The man at my right smiled at me. "You'll like the tale of the Hairy Hands at Postbridge. Once a motorcyclist was killed on the road past Bellever Woods between Two Bridges and Postbridge. Two boys, who were thrown from the sidecar but survived, claimed that the Hairy Hands pushed the bike off the road. On another occasion, a woman sleeping in a caravan said the Hairy Hands reached through the open window and tried to strangle her. They drink strong cider in these parts, you see."

Another guest said, "You've no doubt heard of the Wisht Hounds of Wistman's Wood that Conan Doyle immortalized in *The Hound of the Baskervilles.* The wood is supposed to be the most haunted place on Dartmoor. All the trees are stunted and warped into weird shapes, and at night the Hounds emerge in full cry, led by the Devil on a black horse. The dogs have blazing red eyes, and people unlucky enough to see them are doomed to die within the year." Actually, I had heard that one, but there are so many different versions of folk tales, it's always fascinating to hear another one.

The doctor across the table asked if I knew the legend of Kitty Jay, and when I shook my head, she said, "It's not a happy reflection on the social attitudes of the day, I'm afraid. Two hundred years ago, Kitty was an orphan, apprenticed to a farmer at Holne, not far from the route sailors used to walk from their ship at Brixham on the south coast to catch another ship at Barnstaple in the north. When Kitty became pregnant, seduced either by a sailor or by the farmer's son, she dared not confess to the farmer's wife, as she would be thrown out in disgrace, so she took the only course that seemed open to her and hanged herself in the barn. As a suicide she could not, of course, be buried in consecrated ground. She was laid in a grave in a bit of no-man's land at the junction of three parishes near Hound Tor. She was buried in a fetal position, with a stake through her heart so her ghost would not 'walk,' but some say that on a moonlight night, Kitty and her lover can be seen walking along to the inn at Hemsworthy Gate."

A hush fell over the company, broken by Stella, who said quietly, "The legend goes that fresh flowers magically appear each day on Kitty Jay's grave, and visitors often leave money there so the flowers may be renewed. We visited the grave once, do you remember, Oliver? There was only a sprig of withered holly by the stone."

Oliver looked slightly rattled, then recovered with a quick nod. "Of course, darling, I remember. You left a shilling, did you not?"

Stella's face was shadowed. "A shilling? Yes."

I knew Stella and Oliver had wanted children and grieved when none came along. Now, to hide her emotion, Stella lightened the atmosphere with a glittering smile. "How long ago that must have been— before the money changed!"

And the conversation wandered into amusing stories of the general resentment that ensued when the old coins were turned into decimal pence.

After dinner, when we moved back to the drawing room for coffee, a lively discussion of the problems facing the local farmers made me realize that Oliver, for all that he looked like a matinee idol, was not only a clever solicitor but was very much part of the local scene. The Bascombs had for several generations held substantial tracts of land in the moor, raising sheep and one or two crops. I had learned to my surprise that the moor was almost entirely privately owned in spite of being designated as a National Park, an anomaly uncommon in the States.

It was soon clear that Oliver and Stella were actively concerned in the management of their land and keenly aware of the needs of the farming community. I began to see why Oliver might indeed be a frontrunner in the selection process of the Conservative Party.

At a pause in the conversation, the deaf gentleman abruptly turned to Oliver and shouted, "What about this murdered girl, Bascomb? She was an assistant in your office, was she?"

There was a moment of frozen silence. Then Stella's frown was instantly erased and Oliver showed not even a quiver. With an easy smile, he raised his voice without seeming to do so and replied that Darla Brown had indeed been his temporary receptionist the summer before but that he had scarcely known the girl. "A dreadful tragedy," he concluded, to a discreet chorus of assent, the old gentleman nodding with the rest.

As we drove back into Morbridge at the end of the

evening, I remarked to Bea that I thought Oliver's chances for selection must be excellent.

Bea nodded. "I believe the short list—the final three candidates—is to be announced soon, and Oliver's very likely to be on it, I should think. He's been working toward this for years, you know. He's very much in demand as a speaker, and in the last election, he stood for a quite hopeless seat that had been Labour for eons, and this helped his prospects enormously."

"Do you mean that *losing* an election is a step up?"

"Oh, yes, dear. I know it sounds odd, but you see, it gave him the experience of the campaign, and best of all, he garnered more votes than previous members of his party had done for some time."

I smiled. "Stella would be in her element in Westminster. I can see her charming everyone from the P.M. down to the members of the tabloid press."

But when I lay in bed that night, it wasn't Oliver and Stella and their prospects that filled my mind. As I waited for Milton's dewy-feathered sleep to do its job, it was the vision of little Kitty Jay, pregnant, unloved, hopeless, that hovered there in the darkness.

Kitty hadn't had the option of choice. Moralists would say she knew what she did was wrong and she paid the price. Yet, would they ask themselves what Kitty's life was like? The man, whoever he was, may have provided the only affection the girl had ever known.

I thought of all those Victorian novelists who had dealt variously with the so-called "fallen" woman. Some, like Charles Dickens, had understandably copped out by treating their Little Emilys with sympathy, then banishing them to the colonies or killing them off, to avoid offending their readers. Some decades later, as attitudes began to change, Wilkie

Collins had treated these "fallen leaves" with more open compassion. By the end of the century, Thomas Hardy was able not only to make Tess of the d'Urbervilles the poignant heroine of the novel but to outrage some segments of the public by adding the subtitle: "A Pure Woman."

My author, Mary Louise Talbot, had gone as far as her publishers would allow to defend these women, but in the 1860s and '70s the tide of public opinion still ran strongly against her, and her young victims often met untimely deaths.

For little Kitty Jay, there had been no mercy. No wonder the ghosts of the girl and her lover walked the moor at night.

6

THE NEXT MORNING, I HAD PROMISED TO GO TO CHURCH with Bea, while Sally, who usually groaned and begged off, surprised us by announcing she would come along.

"We're studying the nineteenth-century religious movements, Beebee, and yours is terribly high church, isn't it? I can put it into my essay."

I wasn't sure how Bea would feel about this clinical approach to her beliefs, but she seemed happy that Sally was coming, whatever the reason. Did she still hope for a conversion? Poor darling. Miles hadn't attended church for years, and Bea knew I was going along only to please her. Sally didn't look to me like a hot prospect, but who knew what wild dream lurked in her grandmother's head?

The service, as traditional as Sally expected, was sparsely attended by a congregation mostly so elderly that Bea seemed one of the younger members. I enjoyed the singing of the mass, but when the priest stepped forward before the sermon to make a special plea for money to combat the deplorable practice of counseling young women to terminate their unwanted pregnancies, I knew it was all up with Sally. At home in California, she had marched in rallies to preserve a woman's right to choice and had proudly told her friends that in enlightened England, that right was widely available on the National Health, which meant that poor women were not excluded.

As the service went on, my thoughts wandered to Darla Brown. According to the postmortem, her pregnancy was nine or ten weeks advanced. Still plenty of time to terminate if she'd wanted to. Was she, on the other hand, happy about it? She and the unknown boyfriend had planned to marry, perhaps were already married. I must ask Neil if they had checked applications for marriage licenses. At least, they might learn the man's name.

When the church service came to a close, we walked home through a misty rain, Sally looking glum. Over our salad lunch, she was uncharacteristically silent, but when I poured the coffee, she could bear it no longer. Looking at Bea speculatively, she burst out, "So, Beebee, what do you think should happen if *I* became pregnant?"

Bea looked startled. "Oh, dear, I hope that wouldn't happen."

Sally snapped, "Of course, we all hope it wouldn't happen, but what if it *did?*"

Bea's eyes filled with tears. "Oh, darling, I don't know. It's so troubling—"

"But, Beebee, you have to live in the world as it is, don't you?"

Bea shook her head. "I don't think I like the world as it is. We seem to have lost so much that was once of value."

I quoted, "'Wandering between two worlds, one dead, the other powerless to be born.'"

"What's that from, Mums?"

"Matthew Arnold." I noticed I seemed to have old Matthew on the brain. "He went up into the Alps to visit the Carthusian monks and found himself envying the certainty of their faith, although he couldn't share it."

I could see Sally about to make a sharp retort, until a look at Bea's face stopped her. Quietly, she got up and put her arms around her grandmother's neck. "Sorry, Beebee, it's OK."

I must have done something right with the kid, I thought.

A ring at the doorbell produced Jason Trask, tall, gangly, pimply. Sally made the introductions and went off to pack up her gear, taking Bea with her.

"Coffee, Jason?"

"Yes, thank you very much."

"Sally tells me you've read some of M. L. Talbot's work?"

"Yes, but I know almost nothing about her life. There's a tiny squib in the D.N.B. but that's all I've seen."

I smiled. "And the *Dictionary of National Biography* doesn't tell the full story, as you can imagine. She had a pretty stormy childhood, at least financially speaking. Her father was from a so-called 'good' family in Cornwall, but he was a wandering wastrel, to say the least. He brought Mary and her mother up to London and promptly left them there while he pursued the roving life. He turned up now and then with money in his pocket but soon took off again, leaving Mary and her mother to live in genteel poverty, at times in actual hunger."

Jason said indignantly, "And ladies couldn't just go out and find a job. It wasn't done."

"Exactly. But when Mary was nineteen, she decided she'd had enough of this nonsense and joined a theatrical troupe. The family members were horrified, but Mary's mother was a spirited Irish lady who backed her up and traveled everywhere with her as her chaperone."

"Was she a famous actress?"

"No, I'm afraid not. She was attractive rather than beautiful, and for the most part she played character roles rather than ingenues. The pay in provincial theaters wasn't all that great, but their lives were vastly improved over waiting for Papa to turn up and dole out a few pounds."

"How long was she on the stage?"

"About three years. Then she started writing fiction and hit the jackpot with her first novel."

"What about her personal life?"

"That's even more sensational, at least for her day. She fell in love with a man whose mentally-ill wife was confined to a sanatorium, and she lived with him for years until the wife's death enabled them to marry. They had five children of their own and Mary also cared for his four children."

Jason grinned. "I can see why the D.N.B. might leave out the gory details. I'm certainly looking forward to reading your book when it comes out, Mrs. Camden."

I laughed. "We should both live so long, Jason."

We chatted on about Talbot's work and about what Jason was reading this term at the university, until Sally came in, back in her usual jeans and pullover, bookbag over her shoulder.

She stooped to give me a kiss. "We're off, Mums.

We'll see the bog where William found the body and then head back to the university."

My dinner with Neil Padgett that evening took a turn I hadn't expected. He had suggested we take advantage of the glorious weather and drive down to Torquay to a restaurant he liked, overlooking the bay.

As our table was in a secluded corner, with no one nearby, I thought it safe to ask how the case was going. Neil shook his head, and it was pretty clear he was down in the old slough of despond.

"We can't find a lead anywhere at the moment. We're trying to get a picture of what Darla Brown was like. What emerges from her friends at the comprehensive school is that she had plenty of boyfriends but went from one to another, not sticking to one for more than a few weeks at most. There were none too subtle hints from some of the fellows that she liked sex when she was in the mood, but don't try it on if she wasn't, although they didn't put it in those terms. The girlfriends were divided into the envious onlookers and those who liked her high spirits."

"What about her teachers?"

"It seems she made fairly good marks and passed enough of her O levels to go on, but couldn't be persuaded to try for A levels. She was sometimes impudent in class, according to some of her teachers, while others found her prone to daydreaming. None knew her outside of class."

"Did any of her friends know why she went off to London?"

"Not a clue. In fact, soon after leaving school, she seems to have faded from their lives. It's true, the comprehensive is in Kings Abbey rather than in Morbridge, but that's not far enough away to discourage continuing friendships. Yet the boys who rang her up were brushed off, and the girls found her unresponsive and drifted away."

"Some new interest, one would suppose."

"Exactly. But no one seems to know what she was up to. Her mother obviously was not in her confidence, and when we asked the young sister—as you suggested—she clammed up and said Darla never told her anything. The whole case is a dead end."

I told Neil about meeting Sally's friend Jason Trask and asked if they had learned anything about Darla from him.

"Not much. The officer who interviewed him said Jason certainly admired the girl, that was plain enough, but he sensed an undercurrent of resentment somewhere."

"Sally thinks Jason was enamored. Could be she rejected him. He's a brainy kid but not much to look at."

"Yes, very likely. He spoke of being her special friend, and he certainly had no good word for the parents. He used to hang about the house a good deal, and he claims the stepfather is a clod and the mother a nagging shrew."

"Of course, plenty of teenagers would describe all parents that way, but from what we saw at the inquest, I'd say he was right, wouldn't you? Incidentally, I hear you want to talk to Harriet Thorne, another escapee to London. Her grandmother hasn't heard from her for some time." And I told Neil about my meeting with Mabel Thorne and my promise to check up on Harriet's last lodgings.

He said, "Our man in London confirmed she had moved out, leaving no address. If you find her, do let me know. As I recall from the officer's report, the grandmother denied that Harriet saw much of Darla in London, but any lead is better than none. Do you think the grandmother's right?"

"Hard to tell. Mrs. Thorne is rather an ice cube and she obviously didn't care much for Darla. I doubt if Harriet would engage in girlish confidences with her grandmother about Darla, even if there were any. But Neil, what if something's happened to Harriet? She left her job and her bedsitter and suddenly stopped writing."

Neil looked troubled. "These are the most difficult kinds of cases. There's no evidence of foul play. The girl promised to send her new address and presumably hasn't got round to it. But if her body is found somewhere, there's a great hue and cry. Why wasn't she reported missing? Why didn't the police investigate? If the grandmother files a report, then of course the Metropolitan Police in London will get onto it."

"Yes, I see."

I asked if they had thought of looking for a marriage application for Darla Brown and the unknown lover, and saw Neil's mouth turn up in an ironic smile that was exceedingly attractive.

"Yes, Sherlock, that did cross the great minds of the CID. Darla lived in a bedsit in Earl's Court, so they checked Kensington and Chelsea first, as the application must be in the borough where at least one of the parties resides. Then they checked the registry offices of all the inner London boroughs. No luck. We're assuming the boyfriend lived somewhere in the city, but of course he could conceivably live anywhere."

As we talked on about this and that, I was startled to find myself feeling a decided stirring of the old black magic in the quiet charm of this man. Maybe it was that ironic smile, with its affectionate amusement, that had made my heart turn. Maybe it was time to stop comparing every man I met with Miles.

My husband had been all quicksilver dazzle, always the center of every conversation, the star around whom others circled. He used to tell me I was his ornament. "You have only to sit there looking beautiful, Claire," he would say with his ravishing smile, "a jewel in my crown." Now I noticed that the stab I always felt when I remembered Miles glimmered painlessly away as I watched Neil's face light with enthusiasm over a point of particular interest or shift from glinting humor to contemplation.

After dinner, we walked along a promenade overlooking the bay, and finally settled on a bench as darkness fell, inhaling the summer-promising air.

Abruptly, Neil said, "Janice rang up yesterday. We're getting the final agreements ready in the divorce."

I said nothing, realizing how little I knew about his marriage. Vaguely I remembered his wife from the party in London—a pretty, dark-haired woman. I didn't ask what this had to do with me. Obviously, he needed to talk.

"She went off last summer, soon after I had the offer to come here to Devon. She said she had no intention of being trapped in darkest Africa, but I believe she was looking for a reason. She went back for a time to stay with her family, who have a place in Hertfordshire. Daddy amuses himself when he isn't golfing by sitting on boards and pontificating about the responsibilities of the landowner."

Neil stopped, staring out at lights of the harbor, while I waited in silence. "Janice and I met sixteen years ago when I was detective inspector, and she was entranced to meet an intellectual policeman, as she put it. Afterward, I learned she had been hopelessly in love with some ne'er-do-well baronet who dropped her for someone else. Janice was already thirty, and suitors were not exactly swarming. When she saw I was interested, she set out to make it a match. At least, that's the way I saw it afterward. At the time, I thought I had won first prize at the fair."

Neil paused, then went on. "Of course, she was always aware she married out of her class. I should have known better from the beginning. You see, I grew up with a mother who felt she had married beneath her. My father was a country policeman with a lot of Yorkshire in his speech, who never advanced out of uniform. My mother, whose father was a school-master, insisted on sending me to the 'right' schools and keeping my speech as pure as her own. Having a degree from the university at Bristol has helped my career, but it cut no ice with Janice and her crowd, who thought 'redbricks' were terribly amusing."

I was tempted to make some nasty remark about the British and their insufferable class distinctions until I remembered that Americans are not immune to playing the same game. I'd seen what a nest of faculty wives could do to the simple country girl who had married out of high school and slaved to help her husband through his doctoral dissertation.

We sat in silence for a while. Then Neil stood up. "Shall we?"

I nodded, and we sauntered slowly back to his car.

On the drive back to Morbridge we reverted to small talk, but both of us were perfectly aware of the unspoken declaration going on below the surface.

As we stood at Bea's door, Neil said, "You're going up to London tomorrow?"

"Yes."

"I'll be up in a few days. I'll see you then."

He put both hands on my shoulders, and I reached for his face. The first kiss was gentle, tentative. The second was not.

BARTHOLOMEW HOUSE

The gun told him she was dead... too late
for Mr. Smith to save her. Laughing. The
Mr. Smith.

7

BEA HAD BEEN SCHEDULED TO TAKE MABEL THORNE TO THE doctor the next morning, but when she came down for breakfast red-nosed and coughing, I sent her back to bed with her cold remedies. "I'm stopping at Mabel's to talk about her granddaughter anyhow," I said. "I'll take her on to her appointment."

Even for this street of fine old houses, the Thorne place loomed in splendor, gabled and chimneyed to a fare-thee-well. It looked like the home of a woman of means, but I knew that meant nothing in today's world. Bea had wondered if Mabel's income would be sufficient in the event of a prolonged illness, but it wasn't a question she could ask of someone like Mabel.

I brought my car up the drive as close to the front door as I could get, and following directions, went through the unlocked door, turning left out of the hall to a room so dark I could scarcely see the figure sitting bolt upright in a wing chair.

"How very kind of you to come, Mrs. Camden. Please sit down." Mabel's speech sounded like something out of an Edwardian novel, but I knew it was perfectly natural to her.

"Thank you."

"I cannot offer you refreshment, as my home helper does not come until the afternoon on Mondays."

"It's quite all right, thank you. I've just finished breakfast."

Mabel handed me a sheet of notepaper. "I have here Harriet's last address in London."

I cleared my throat. "I don't wish to alarm you, Mrs. Thorne, but have you thought of reporting your granddaughter as a missing person?"

"Yes, but I believe such a move to be premature. The police have no doubt already enquired at this address, as they wish to question Harriet about Darla Brown. Since they have evidently learned nothing, I shall wait another week or so before taking further action. I may have a letter from her meanwhile."

"I don't know if I can find out anything the police have missed."

"Sometimes people are reluctant to talk with police but will do so with a pleasant lady like yourself."

I smiled. "Yes, I see."

"I asked you to come here, Mrs. Camden, because I thought there might be something among Harriet's effects that would assist you. Her room is on the floor above my own, and I have not attempted the second flight of stairs for some time. I believe she took a minimum of her belongings with her to London, not knowing how long she might remain. If you would care to have a look, I would be most grateful."

Back in the cavernous hall, I climbed two flights of stairs, went down a corridor of closed doors, and found Harriet's room under the central gable over-looking the street. I drew back the heavy drapes from the dormer windows to let in some light. A dreary room, I thought. A bed in one corner, covered with a plain brown spread, a monstrous wardrobe of dark mahogany, a modern plastic-topped desk, gray carpet. So different from Sally's room at home in California, with its white-ruffled canopy bed, the stuffed animals from childhood, the stereo, the books, the Renoir reproductions on the walls.

I didn't see much to tell me about Harriet herself, except for an enormous poster tacked to the wall opposite the bed, depicting a clown-like figure, distorted but attractive, reminiscent of early Picasso. The name of the painter, Nikolai Nevsky, rang a bell. Then I remembered. In London the other day, reading the newspaper to check what was on in the metropolis, I had seen a notice of a forthcoming exhibit of Nevsky and two other young painters somewhere in London —the Hayward Gallery, maybe? I wondered if Harriet had tried her hand at painting.

Gazing at the barren room, I debated how far I should take her grandmother's permission to look around. I felt awkward about opening the drawers of the desk. Yet if something had happened to the girl, it might be important to learn something about her. If she really was missing, the police wouldn't hesitate to search everything. Okay. I rationalized, if I find anything embarrassing to her, I'll just keep quiet about it.

I needn't have worried. The desk revealed no significant secrets. Harriet had probably done a thorough cleanup before leaving for London, for the drawers were tidy and half-empty. A box of letterpaper, pens and pencils, paper clips, a few school papers; an embroidery hoop circling what looked to be a dresser cover, with the letters "MO" in bright blue cross-stitch, the needle still stuck in the unfinished work; some newspaper clippings about the artist Nevsky. No letters or postcards, no address book or list of phone numbers.

Then, in the bottom drawer, I found a photo album. No baby pictures. The first snaps showed a plain girl of nine or ten at the seaside, a grim-looking Mabel in the background under an umbrella. Annual visits to what looked like the same place were interspersed with occasional pictures of Harriet, at a school picnic, at church outings, and in her white dress for Confirmation.

Then came Harriet in her early teens, with her straight brown hair and stodgy body, posed with a hockey stick, or standing unsmiling outside the church.

Few friends appeared in the pictures until I turned a page and came upon Darla Brown, her mass of blond hair flying, her body poured into tight jeans and a pullover. The news photos hadn't half done her justice. The girls must have been fifteen or sixteen, I guessed, when Darla appeared in the album, and thereafter every page had pictures of her. Many of the snaps had evidently been taken at the Browns' cottage, for sometimes the younger sister or brother appeared in the background, and once Mrs. Brown posed with Darla by a kitchen sink. Only a few snaps showed the two girls together, Darla's vibrance making Harriet seem all the more placid.

Certainly, Harriet had seen more of Darla than her grandmother knew, yet Darla's friends at the comprehensive school had not regarded Harriet as a particular friend. It was easy enough to read. At home in

Morbridge, Darla tolerated Harriet's hanging about, but at school, her other friends took precedence. I doubted if things were much different in London. An occasional visit from Harriet, perhaps, when Darla had nothing more compelling to do.

I slipped out a recent snapshot of Harriet, then closed the album, laid it back in the drawer, and went down the stairs. No point in mentioning the snapshots to her grandmother.

As I helped Mabel into my car, it seemed to me she had grown markedly weaker in the few days since I'd seen her last. I knew she had been unable to attend church on Sunday. Now I saw, in the grayish pallor of her skin and the dark hollows under her eyes, the marks of serious illness.

As we drove, I asked if Harriet had shown any aptitude for painting or drawing, and got only a puzzled look from Mabel. "No. Why do you ask?"

When I mentioned the Nikolai Nevsky poster, her face cleared. "Oh, yes, to be sure. A year or so ago, Harriet attended an exhibition of paintings in Exeter, where Mr. Nevsky was present. She was very much taken with his work and talked enthusiastically about him for some time. He gave her what I believe is known as an autograph, which pleased her very much, though I fail to comprehend why simply obtaining a signature should be a source of such gratification."

Poor Harriet, I thought. She finally got excited about something, only to get a frigid response from her grandmother.

At the health center, I helped Mabel to a chair, where she sat, leaning on her cane for support. She had urged me to leave her, saying she could call for a taxi when she was ready to go, but I knew the vagaries of small-town taxis and assured her I had plenty of time and would see her home.

My virtue was rewarded, for instead of the long wait I expected, she was called within five minutes, and the attractive young receptionist took her arm to help her into the surgery.

Presently, finding a tattered magazine on cricket less than absorbing, I watched the young woman as she handled phone calls for the three doctors in the practice, pulled the patients' folders from the large file cabinet at my right, and gave cheery greetings to those coming in.

A pregnant young woman came in and took a chair near the desk, saying to the receptionist, "Isn't it dreadful about poor Darla?"

"Yes, too awful. Did you know the police questioned me about her?"

"Oh, dear! What did you say?"

"Not much. Darla dropped by here to say hello when she was down last month, but she didn't say *anything* about getting married, like it said in the news. She seemed very excited and happy, but when I said let's have lunch, she just looked mysterious and said she couldn't. It was a really busy day here—they had me on the hop—and next thing I knew, she had gone."

I could see why Neil hadn't bothered to mention this interview. The fact that Darla couldn't lunch with her friend because she had other plans didn't exactly advance the investigation. It would help a lot more if they had found out who she *did* have lunch with, but evidently they had not.

A few minutes later, the receptionist was called to help Mabel to the door, while I brought the car up. On the brief drive, she looked exhausted, and when we arrived, she let me help her into the house, where she lay back against the cushions on a sofa in the sitting room and even let me get her a cup of tea. I saw a little color come into her face as the hot liquid did its work.

With the assurance that her helper would come later to prepare her lunch, I left and started on the drive back to London.

8

IT WAS EARLY AFTERNOON WHEN I DROVE INTO THE CITY.
The plain sailing along the motorway came to an
abrupt halt when the M-4 ended, and I began slogging
my way through the traffic. Over a quick lunch at a
services stop off the motorway, I had looked up
Harriet's last address in my trusty *A to Z* and found
the street in the area beyond Notting Hill, behind the
Queensway tube stop. Deciding it was easier to look it
up now than to battle my way back again tomorrow, I
reached the Bayswater Road and found Trefford Place
easily enough. I passed some once-grand houses with
double-pillared fronts, still well-kept and offering
luxury flats, but those at Harriet's end of the road
were dreary with flaking paint and bare patches where
gardens had once flourished.

On the card at the door, "H. Thorne" had been
crossed out for number nine and something illegible
scribbled underneath. Inside in the hall, I saw two
letters on the table addressed to Harriet, postmarked
Devon and dated within the past two weeks. Pretty

sure they were from her grandmother, I looked for the return address but found none. Not too surprising, for only in recent years had people in England begun to include the sender's address on the envelope, a practice much too modern for Mabel, I'd have guessed. It was also obvious that Harriet had left no forwarding address. Nothing to do but leave the letters where they were.

I mounted the stairs, finding number nine two flights up. No one at home there. I knocked on the adjoining doors and had no luck there either. Most of the tenants would be at work. I might have to come back in the evening after all.

Then a door opened across the passage and an elderly woman's face appeared in the space permitted by the chain on her door. I gave her a smiling "Hello" and asked if I might speak to her.

"You from Social Services, Miss?" she asked.

"No, I'm just a friend looking for the young lady who lived in number nine."

I held out the snapshot of Harriet for her inspection and the woman nodded. Rattling the chain free, she stood in her doorway, pulling a sweater across her thin bosom. "I heard the police was here asking questions about her, but I was out that day. I don't know nothing about her anyhow. Never spoke to the girl, except good morning and that. An Indian gentleman has the room now."

"Do you know if she had many visitors?"

"Never heard much. She kept herself to herself, I'll say that for her. Not like the ones as has people coming and going at all hours."

"Do you happen to know when she moved out?"

The old woman pulled her sweater closer around her. "I couldn't say to the day. But I remember when she was taking her things down the stairs. It was late—midnight, maybe—and I heard a loud thump on the stairs just here outside my door. I opened the door, leaving the chain in place, and I saw it was the girl in number nine. There was a young man with her, and they was lifting a box between them. She sort of whispers, 'Be careful, Derek,' and he says, 'I got it,' and they goes on down the stairs. Then I didn't hear no more and I went back to bed."

I thanked the woman and turned to go when I saw a black-haired man with the soulful dark eyes of a Pakistani pass me and put a key in the door of number nine.

"Excuse me—"

The man looked at me in surprise. "Yes?"

"I was looking for the young lady who formerly lived in number nine. Do you mind my asking how long you have had the room?"

"I am here almost four weeks. I never meet the person who is here before me. When I pay the rent, the man say the lady give notice and move out before her week is up, so I am able to come in at once. Very good for me."

"Yes, I see. Thank you very much."

By the time I got back to my car, the peak hour traffic was on with a vengeance, and I painfully worked my way into Bloomsbury, happy to find a parking spot near the flat and glad I had picked up my resident's parking permit before going down to Devon.

The next morning, before settling down to work, I finished my unpacking and called up a few London friends to say I was back. The transition was easy enough, as I had for years divided my life comfortably between California and London. The flat in Bedford Square had been in the Camden family since the time of Miles's grandparents, a spacious affair, with three bedrooms and a study overlooking the square. I'd always loved it and was glad it was allotted to me in the divorce proceedings.

Coming back was getting easier. Time seemed to have fed that natural spring of adaptability that humans are endowed with, and after the early months of anger and resentment, I could reflect on the past with some degree of tranquillity.

In the early years of our marriage, when I had offered to abandon my career and come to live in London, Miles had smilingly refused. "I quite like our comings and goings," he would say. Should I have seen that as a portent? I don't think so. Looking back, I believe Miles did try to make a success of our marriage.

We had married in California, where he had come for the ceremony granting my final degree. We'd met in London the summer before, spending a giddy three months of delight for me, and, I had thought, for him too. The year passed in a whirl of letters, phone calls, transatlantic flights.

When, after the graduation ceremony, Miles said quite suddenly, "Let's be married here in California, darling," I assented without a shadow of doubt. We spent the summer in London, and I went back to teach at the university at South Coast, where I'd been hired on tenure track in the English department. When Sally was on the way, I took an unpaid leave and stayed on in London for a time after she was born, before going back to teaching. Two years later, Miles took a leave from the Home Office and stayed with me for some months in South Coast. And so it went, with many months apart but always intervals together at holidays and summers.

Miles adored Sally, and maybe the break would

have come sooner except for his fear of losing her affection. To be fair, he was reluctant to hurt me too.

Oh, well, time to put it aside and get back to work.

Thoughts of Neil Padgett glimmered pleasantly on the periphery as I settled down in front of my word processor. Surrounded by notes and reference books, I felt like Alice walking through the looking-glass. My teaching life, with its consuming pressures, was behind me for a year, and now I could get on with my other existence.

In her fiction, my author, Mary Louise Talbot, had had to cater to Victorian public prudery if she expected to get published, and I was interested in examining the ways in which Talbot, like many of her contemporaries, managed to slip in nuggets of social criticism without offending her readers.

As I had told Jason Trask, Talbot was no shrinking violet. In her own personal life, she had spurned a good many social conventions, a freedom denied to the characters in her novels. In the opening chapters of the biography, already completed, I had covered her early life, her years on the stage, and the success of her first novel, inspired by the enormous popularity of Wilkie Collins's *The Woman in White,* which came out in 1859. Labelled by the critics as another "sensation novelist," Mary cheerfully collected her money and ignored their jibes.

I had now reached the point in Talbot's life when she and her lover, along with Mary's mother, had taken a house big enough for all of them, including his children, and Mary was writing her second novel, *The Specimen,* which would become another bestseller and remain one of her best-known works.

The title of the novel referred to the death of a young woman whose body was pierced by an arrow as she sat at the foot of a tree, thus pinning her to the tree trunk like a human "specimen." The archery craze was in full swing at the time, everyone practicing enthusiastically with bow and arrow. It was assumed at first that the death had been an accident, and the novel generates plenty of suspense before the final solution is revealed. Replete with sub-plots and a large cast of characters, it moves at a leisurely pace by today's standards, for the big money at that time, after serialization, was not from individual sales of books —they were too expensive for the average reader— but from the lending libraries. For decades, writers were under the tyranny of lenders like Mudie's: if a book didn't extend to three fat volumes, it was no dice, as readers had to pay separately for each volume rented, thus boosting the revenue. Cliff-hangers were essential to keep the orders coming in.

The Specimen opens as Emily Spalding, age eighteen, returns home at the close of her schooling at a young ladies' academy, where she was prepared to face the world with skills of embroidery, drawing, music, and the fine art of playing hostess to the husband who would come along in due course.

Tartly, Tallbot writes, "Having lost her mother in childhood, Emily had little experience of parental affection. Her father was a distant figure who now and then remembered her existence long enough to give her a vague pat on the head, but having no one else to love, Emily believed herself devoted to him."

It took a long time for that devotion to waver. A Victorian gentleman of considerable wealth, Mr. George Spalding lived at Hazelwood, his country house in Surrey, and pursued a life of comfortable indolence. Having no son, Spalding had developed a vaguely paternal fondness for his neighbor, Sir Wilfred Probis, often giving the younger man advice on matters of finance.

Sir Wilfred had fallen victim to the craze for do-it-yourself science that was fashionable at the time, and all visitors to Probis Hall were given a tour of his "workroom," where shelves of stuffed birds and glass-encased insects were carefully labelled and catalogued.

When Emily Spalding returned from school, Sir Wilfred noticed that she was no longer a child but had grown into an attractive young woman. Now in his thirties, he evidently decided it was time to marry, and at his first hint on the subject, Spalding exclaimed, "Of course, you shall have her!"

With fine irony, Talbot writes, "What could be more suitable? George Spalding saw no reason why Emily's wishes should be consulted. It was a splendid prospect for the girl, and her natural duty to her father made refusal unthinkable."

When Emily protested that she did not love Sir Wilfred, her father cried, "Not love him? Pah! You'll like him well enough once you're married. He's a splendid fellow. Let's hear no more of this. You will, of course, speak to no one on this subject until the matter is resolved."

A year earlier, Emily might have meekly acquiesced, but now there had been a change in her life which she could not divulge to her father, having scarcely acknowledged it to herself. On her return from school, a music master had been engaged, on the recommendation of the headmistress, to continue Emily's instruction in singing, as this had been her most promising accomplishment. The arrival of Stephen Ward, an attractive young man of twenty-two, might have signalled danger to any parent with normal powers of observation, but to Mr. Spalding, the music master was little better than a servant and therefore non-existent.

In the month or so of Stephen Ward's residence at Hazelwood, he had fallen in love with his pupil, though no word had crossed his well-bred lips, for he knew that, penniless as he was, his passion was hopeless. Emily was equally enamored, and equally silent. In a series of charming scenes, Talbot had sketched in their growing attachment, as they took afternoon walks through the softly folded green of the Surrey countryside or sang duets which became increasingly charged with unspoken emotion.

Emily's only confidante was her cousin Annette, who had come to live at Hazelwood on the death of her father in the preceding year. During Emily's school holidays, she had found in Annette the sister she had always longed for and with whom she could now speak haltingly of her admiration for Stephen Ward.

Annette, a year the elder, saw the picture whole and without sentiment. "Any fool can see he adores you, Emily," she told her cousin, "but it's no good, you know. Uncle would never consent. Our world is ruled by money, my dear, and poor Stephen hasn't got any."

She might have added, "Nor have I." Annette's father, a cousin of George Spalding, was one of those ne'er-do-well fathers that cropped up regularly in Talbot's novels and for whom the author reserved her bitterest scorn. Plainly, there were echoes of Talbot's own childhood in the scenes of Annette growing up with a father who was a con artist and who had spent what little money they had on fine clothes for himself while his daughter went shabbily dressed.

The luxury of life at Hazelwood, while welcome for its comforts, was galling to Annette as a constant reminder of her dependence. Her cousin George Spalding—"Uncle" was a courtesy title—treated her with the arrogance of the rich man patronizing a poor relation. Only her affection for Emily gave her consolation. . . .

In my Bloomsbury flat, the phone rang, jolting me out of Mary Louise Talbot's world into my own.

Neil Padgett. "Claire, I expect to be in London tomorrow. Are you free in the evening?"

"Yes, fine."

"I don't know the time. I can give you a ring when the schedule sorts itself out. Will that do?"

"Yes, of course."

"Right. Till tomorrow, then."

A commonplace conversation, one would have thought, but charged with anticipation for both of us.

By lunchtime, I had checked some references and read again through several journal articles I had photocopied, astonished as always that more than four hours had passed. As there was no food in the flat yet, I'd treat myself to lunch out, then do my shopping.

Over my lasagne at a local bistro, I opened the *Guardian* to the Arts page, read a review of a new play which I decided to see even though the reviewer took a few snide potshots at its lead actor, and saw the notice of the three young artists whose work was on show at the Hayward Gallery. Tonight, the announcement said, Nikolai Nevsky would be there from eight to nine to chat with viewers.

It might be a long shot, I thought, but if Harriet Thorne was still alive—and in London—I'd be willing to bet she would show up. I decided I'd better be there, just in case.

9

BY HALF-PAST SEVEN THAT EVENING, ARMED WITH MY UM-
brella against the usual drizzly rain of early June, I set
off for the Hayward Gallery. No point in driving, as
I'd only lose my convenient parking spot by the time I
got back. I walked over to Southampton Row and took
a bus to the stop on Waterloo Bridge, where I went
down the steps past the massive gray concrete bulk of
the National Theatre and back under the bridge to the
matching structures that together formed the complex
known as the South Bank. The ugliness of the postwar
architecture had not mellowed with time but was
more tolerable here on this side of the Thames, where
it did not stand cheek-by-jowl with buildings of
ancient grandeur, than it was on the other side of the
river, where giant office buildings rose incongruously
around the precincts of St. Paul's Cathedral.

As I emerged from under the bridge, the Hayward
Gallery was on my left, its intimate size suitable for
small exhibitions. At my right, threaded with a maze

of concrete stairs and walkways, were the concert halls, facing the river.

I paid my entrance fee and sauntered through the first rooms, keeping an eye out for anyone who might resemble Harriet Thorne. Of the three artists on display, I found that I preferred Nikolai Nevsky's work to the others. One was very much in the splash-and-splotch school, which I thought was pretty old-hat by this time, while the other was into collage, sticking bits of newspaper, glass, beer labels, and pictures of nude male bodies on rough boards. Nevsky seemed to have at least some talent for drawing, and in addition to his Picasso clowns, he had done some distorted but rather attractive studies of street scenes in vibrant colors.

I looked at my watch. A few minutes after eight. The artist should be here by now, ready to chat with his fans. And now I could hear voices in the last of the rooms and came upon a crowd of perhaps thirty people, some looking at the paintings that lined the walls, others gathered in a loose grouping around the painter, a short, dark-haired man who appeared to be engaged in a spirited debate with one of the crowd, while others added their opinions to the discussion.

Surreptitiously, I slipped the snapshot of Harriet Thorne out of my handbag, circling the fringes of the group but unable to see clearly over the shifting heads. Someone pressed behind me, and turning, I saw a young man in a zippered jacket, his head a mat of tightly curling brownish hair. Pushing past me, he burrowed his way into the group, while I moved toward the side, the better to see faces rather than backs of heads.

Now I noticed that Curlytop was speaking intently to a young woman whose straight dark hair fell below her shoulders. As she turned to look back toward where I had been standing, I got a full view of her face. No doubt about it. It was Harriet Thorne.

Starting to work my way through the crowd, I saw with surprise that the girl had turned away from the artist and was moving quickly back out of the group. With a ruthless shove or two, I slipped past and caught up with her as she made for the door.

"Harriet!"

The girl turned and looked back at me, and in that brief moment I saw two things that surprised me. The first was that Harriet at close range was more attractive than I'd have guessed from the photo album. The creamy skin of her face was adroitly touched with light makeup in the current fashion, and her abundant dark hair swung thickly on her shoulders. She was far from slim. Her jeans, pulled tight over her ample hips, recalled the schoolgirl of the snapshots, but something in the way she moved gave the indefinable sign of a young woman confident of her own sexuality.

More surprising than her appearance, however, was the look she gave me in that fleeting instant before she hurried away. *Her face was white with terror!*

I might have expected irritation or even hostility toward a stranger who accosted her. But why fear? I took a step to follow the girl and found my way blocked by Curlytop, who said, "Excuse me," but didn't budge from the doorway.

I took a long shot. "Are you Derek?"

Startled, he glared at me. "Who the hell are you?"

"Look," I snapped, "if you're a friend of Harriet Thorne, please tell her that her grandmother is worried about her. She's about to call in the police if she doesn't hear from her soon."

I pushed past him and ran through the intervening rooms and out of the gallery, catching a glimpse of a figure under an umbrella walking rapidly away. The drizzle had turned into a vigorous downpour. Water clogged my eyes and clouded my vision as I followed her down the steps between the towering bulk of the Royal Festival Hall and the lesser structure of the Queen Elizabeth Hall. I groped for my umbrella and managed to get it open. Now I could see her, rushing along the walk by the river. It wasn't fully dark yet, but although the heavy rain made it hard to see, I knew it was Harriet, her long hair flying behind her.

At the bottom, she turned left, past the Festival Hall. Where was she going? She might have gone back toward Waterloo Bridge, where buses or taxis were plentiful. There wasn't any place to hide down here, only the broad promenade along the river, with its towering trees. I doubted if she would go into the concert hall, as its lobbies would be deserted while a performance was going on.

Ahead of us, as we sped past the hall, I could hear trains thundering across the Hungerford bridge, which led across the river to Charing Cross station. There was a footpath alongside the tracks, which is handy if you want to get from the South Bank into the Strand. Now I saw that was where she was headed.

Winded and panting, I followed as she started up the long flight of steps to the bridge. After all, I thought, she was Sally's age, and although I tried to keep in shape, I was no fitness freak, and twenty-some years' age difference was bound to take its toll. By the time I made it up the stairs, I noticed with relief that she had slowed her pace and was not looking back to see if I was there. Maybe I could catch her yet.

There were not many people on the bridge at this hour. One or two umbrellas passed me going in the other direction on the narrow walkway, and looking back, I saw a few figures coming along behind. To my right, the dark water of the river rolled grimly, far below the metal rail.

Summoning all my strength, I decided to try for a quick sprint that would bring me close enough to call out to Harriet, when a train chose that moment to come rattling and roaring along the near track at my left. Oh, well, I thought, if I stick with her till she takes a bus or the tube, I'll have a fair chance of speaking to her again, perhaps learning where she lives.

I had no warning of what happened next. I heard no footsteps behind me. I only knew that something struck the back of my head and I fell. Then rough hands yanked my shoulder bag off my arm. My automatic shriek of fright was submerged by the thunder of the train.

Stunned with shock, I lay with my face in a shallow puddle and heard voices above me.

"Are you all right, miss?"

"He went straight on, the bastard."

Arms helped me to my feet, retrieved my umbrella, and opened it against the still pouring rain.

A man coming in the other direction held out my handbag. "Is this yours, then?"

"Yes, thank you so much."

Shaking, I took the bag and saw the zipper was open and the billfold gone.

The man and woman who had been some distance behind me and had seen the mugging walked with me across the bridge.

I asked, "Can you describe the man?" and they both shook their heads.

The man said, "We only saw his back. His cap was pulled down. Wore jeans and an anorak."

The woman added, "I believe he was young—twenties, I should think."

When we reached Charing Cross, they wished me good luck and went on their way.

I found a phone, dialed "999," and was met at the front of the station by an officer who took the information and drove me back to the flat, as I had no money for a taxi.

After a strong drink and a hot bath, I rang up Bea in Morbridge to say she could tell Mrs. Thorne I had seen Harriet. I didn't mention the attack on the bridge. No use worrying her.

Still, like a child, I wanted to be consoled, and I rang up a couple of friends, hoping to share my sad story. I got an answering machine for one and no answer for the other.

Then I thought of Neil Padgett. He'd given me his home number in Devon, and on an impulse, I dialed. As the double rings went unanswered, I reflected that a policeman could hardly be expected to ooze sympathy over such a trivial crime as this one. Better to hang up than receive a figurative pat on the head. About to drop the receiver, I heard Neil's voice. "Padgett here."

Keeping it light, I described finding Harriet Thorne at the Hayward and what had happened on the bridge. "The wretch got away with fifty pounds in cash and made me lose Harriet!"

I couldn't have been more wrong about Neil. He oozed sympathy in a most gratifying manner. "What a rotten thing to happen, Claire." He inquired about every bruise and the small bump on my head, muttering curses against my attacker, and bemoaning the loss of the fifty pounds.

When I pointed out that at least I had found Harriet Thorne alive and well in London but had failed to find out where she was living, I heard his voice take on the humorous tone I liked so much, calling to mind the upturn of his mouth and the flicker of irony in his dark eyes. "Look here, darling, if you carry on like this, we'll have to take out a license for you as a private investigator."

I registered the "darling" and filed it away as we said good-night.

10

BACK AT MY DESK THE NEXT MORNING, I FOUND THAT MY bruises from the attack on the bridge the evening before were causing no problems. I was more angry than hurt. I reported the theft of my bank and credit cards and planned to get a new driver's license that afternoon, and now I could put the whole thing aside and get back to Mary Louise Talbot.

The kind of book I was doing was known in the trade as a critical biography, meaning that the focus would be not only on the events of the author's life but on the works themselves, on their literary qualities and on their significance as social documents of the period. A minor novelist like Talbot had escaped treatment by the excesses of current schools of literary criticism. The Freudians and the Marxists had largely ignored her, there were a couple of perceptive comments in articles by an archetypal critic, and recently there had been some good feminist discussion of her work. As the structuralists faded into the trendy deconstructionists, I tried to steer clear of treacherous currents and paddle along in midstream, sticking to a common-sense approach to my subject.

A major problem for today's readers is to comprehend with compassion the failure of a Victorian heroine to assert herself against parental authority. How could Emily Spalding allow herself to be persuaded into an engagement with Sir Wilfred Probis when she was in love with someone else? For this was what happened in the novel. Theoretically, these young women did have the power of veto. They were rarely chained or beaten into submission. Then why didn't Emily simply tell her father to forget it? Why didn't her cousin Annette, who loved her, tell her to run off with Stephen Ward, the music master, instead of admitting that it was a hopeless cause?

The pressures against such a step were overwhelming. Even if Emily had been willing to live somewhere with Stephen in genteel poverty, she would face not only the wrath of her father, whom she had automatically obeyed from infancy, she would also be cut off from all respectable society. Her friends from school, the neighboring gentry, everyone who had figured at all in her young life would reject her. Stephen himself, who was after all a gentleman, would be unlikely to ask her to take such a step. These acts of sacrifice were not necessarily fictional devices to thwart young love but were grounded in a harsher reality. She could refuse to marry Sir Wilfred, if she had the courage, but she could not thereafter marry Stephen Ward.

The worst of Emily's dilemma was that she could supply no real objection to Sir Wilfred. She had known him since childhood as her father's friend and had liked him well enough in a vague sort of way, although he had taken as little notice of her as her father had. That he was a good-looking man, well-spoken and modest, she could not deny. Even her cousin Annette had admitted to admiring him.

Now she thought to herself wretchedly, why should Sir Wilfred suddenly take an interest in her, finding opportunities to speak with her alone, to present her with trifling gifts of flowers from his garden, or to take her to visit country neighbors, where archery was everywhere the entertainment of choice? Absorbed in her awakening love for the music master, Emily had dreamed her way through these events until startled by her father's announcement that Sir Wilfred wanted to marry her.

She longed to confide her trouble to Annette, but her father had expressly forbidden her to speak of it to anyone until she had "come to her senses" and consented to his wishes. Moreover, Annette had been depressed and moody for some time and Emily did not want to distress her further. Emily knew that during the months her cousin had lived at Hazelwood, Annette had become friends with the steward on the estate, a pleasant, hard-working man named John Travis, who relieved George Spalding of all tiresome responsibilities. Spalding's refrain, "Leave it to Travis," had become a byword in the household.

Travis's son, young Johnny, had developed an adolescent passion for Annette and would sometimes listen to her while ignoring all other advice. Now he was accused by a shopkeeper in the village of stealing a packet of arrows. While archery was officially practiced only by the gentry, Johnny was mad for the game and had been seen practicing with an old bow and some arrows he had found in the barn. There seemed little doubt that the theft had taken place, but Johnny swore he hadn't done it, and no one could find the missing arrows. Annette's powers of persuasion with Johnny had failed, and if the boy should be convicted, he would undoubtedly go to prison. There was little sentimentality about juvenile crime at that period.

So, finding Annette preoccupied, Emily kept her trouble to herself for the time. Her father had pressed her once more to accept Sir Wilfred's offer, ignoring her protests in his usual fashion. It was common enough for young girls to refuse a first offer, so that when George Spalding had told Sir Wilfred that Emily had not at once welcomed the suggestion of marriage, both men assumed this to be maidenly reserve. Thus Sir Wilfred believed he had little cause for concern when he arrived at Hazelwood on an August day of exquisite weather, carrying in his pocket a small velvet box.

Emily sat at the piano in the music room, daydreaming of her music master, who had been called home a few days earlier to an ailing mother, when Sir Wilfred approached and bent over her:

'My dear Emily, I have something for you which I hope you will accept. You know of my wish to make you my wife. I shall do everything in my power to make you happy.'

Emily looked up at the face not two feet from her own. The smooth skin, the black hair flat to the head, the slate-colored eyes, now glinting with emotion, all so familiar to her from childhood, seemed now to belong to a stranger.

Emily drew back but looked directly into his eyes. 'I am sorry, Sir Wilfred.' Her voice broke and she went on in a whisper. 'You see, I don't wish to be married.'

'My dear girl, it is quite understandable. You are very young, and I shall be happy to wait until you have grown accustomed to the notion. I want you simply to wear this as a token of my love for you.'

Sir Wilfred reached into his waistcoat pocket and

produced the velvet box, opening it to reveal an exquisite ring of rubies and diamonds. Raising her left hand
where it lay on the piano, he slipped the ring on her
finger, then bent and kissed her gently on the lips.

Emily drew back her hand, but at this auspicious
moment, George Spalding appeared like a genie out of
a bottle, shook hands vigorously with Sir Wilfred, and
clasped Emily in his arms.

'My dear, dear girl. This makes me very happy. Very
happy indeed!'

'But Papa . . .'

'Yes, yes, very happy indeed. Splendid! Come, Sir
Wilfred, we'll have a toast!' And the two men swept out
of the room, Spalding's arm round the shoulder of the
younger man.

Stunned, Emily sat on the piano bench, her eyes
stinging with tears. She would have to seek out her
father after Sir Wilfred had gone and explain that she
had not consented, that he misunderstood. But what
objection could she give? She had no reason to dislike
the man who had proposed marriage. Her heart thud-
ded painfully at the mere thought of attempting to defy
her father.

Now she realized that were it not for the presence in
her thoughts of Stephen Ward, she would perhaps have
accepted Sir Wilfred, perhaps have come to care for
him, as her father had predicted when the subject first
arose. Was it still possible? She shuddered at the
thought of his kiss, but in truth she knew it was not
because she disliked Sir Wilfred himself but because
she wished so desperately that it had been Stephen who
bent over her and pressed his lips to hers.

Now she must go to Annette and ask her advice.
Never mind her father's injunction. Older by a year,
Annette seemed to Emily immensely wiser than she.
Finding her cousin in the garden, lying listlessly on a

deck chair under a tree, Emily threw herself on the grass and poured out her story.

For a moment, Annette seemed scarcely to take in what Emily was telling her. Her pale face was immobile, her dark eyes glazed and dull. Then, as Emily held out her hand and Annette saw the gleaming ring, she sat up abruptly. 'Sir Wilfred has asked you to marry him?'

'Yes.'

'And you accepted him?'

'No, I did not! I told him I did not wish to be married, and he simply ignored me and put the ring on my finger. Then he—oh, Annette—he kissed me, and at that moment Papa came in and they began congratulating each other as if it were all settled. What shall I do?'

Annette was silent, staring into Emily's face and at the ring on her finger. Then she lay back in her chair and closed her eyes. 'I don't know, dear. I don't know.'

Now Emily noticed the pallor of her cousin's face, the colorless lips and the dark smudges under the eyes. 'Annette, are you ill?'

'Ill? No, no. Perhaps a little. The heat is troublesome.'

'You must come into the house. Let me put you into the library where it is cool.'

Her arm around her cousin's waist, Emily led her into the house, where Annette consented to lie on the sofa in the library, while Emily rang for a cooling drink. When the servant had come and gone, Annette lay back, looking at Emily in silence. Then she put out a hand and grasped her cousin's arm. 'Don't let them do this, Emily. It's wrong. Tell Uncle you refuse!'

'But what reason shall I give?'

Annette's dark eyes caught fire. 'No reason. Just say you will not. Can you do that?'

'I'll try.'

'Good. I'll rest a little now.' And Annette closed her eyes.

Needless to say, when Emily confronted her father and asked him to return the ring to Sir Wilfred, he shouted her down, saying she would cause him the deepest humiliation if she refused his friend. "I won't have it, Emily," he bellowed. "He has put the ring on your finger and there it stays. Let us hear no more of it."

In a passage of tart commentary, Mary Louise Talbot wrote, "Did George Spalding lie awake that night wondering why his daughter did not want to marry their neighbor? Did he ask himself if it was right for him to insist upon a match against her wishes? Certainly not. George Spalding was a man, the head of his household, accustomed to obedience from his servants and his daughter. He was no more a snob than the next man, but marriage to a baronet was not a privilege to be scorned by a girl who knew nothing of the world. He had taken a fancy to Sir Wilfred and looked forward to having him as a son-in-law. To his mind, there was nothing more to be said."

This was about as far as Talbot could go in attacking the status of women in the 1860s without getting blue-pencilled by her editor. She could never, in her fiction, recommend to her heroines the course of action she had taken in her own life, but she could—and did—take every opportunity to do a little acupuncture, prodding her readers with painless needles to question a blind acceptance of the status quo.

In the late afternoon, Sally rang up to ask if I could come down to Devon the next weekend.

"Jason's asked us to go to the annual letterboxers' party at Princetown on Sunday."

"Princetown? There's nothing much there but the prison, is there?"

"That's right. You'll never believe it, but they have their parties at the prison officers' social club."

"Well, it's more or less in the center of Dartmoor, isn't it? I suppose it's convenient for people from all around the area."

"Yes, and also it seems a lot of the prison officers are letterboxers themselves. So, do you want to go?"

"But your date won't want your mother along, will he?"

"Oh, Mums, Jason's just a friend, not a date. Besides, he thinks you're the bees' rollerskates." Sally had been weaned on the Jeeves stories.

I laughed. "That's terribly flattering, but I really should stay here and slave away."

"Okay. Well, think about it."

"I'll do that, darling."

When Neil Padgett came to the flat that evening, we talked a little about the novel *The Specimen*. But not at first. He walked in and said, "I believe this is where we left off," and we kissed for a long time.

It was much later when we talked about literature.

11

BEFORE NEIL ARRIVED AT THE FLAT, I HAD THOUGHT A good deal about how far I wanted this relationship to go. I was no teenager, to be swept away by the impulse of the moment, although I had to admit I felt pretty swept away when we kissed. In the long term, if there was one, it seemed to me marriage was out of the question. With Miles, the long-distance arrangement had been ideal, but I doubted if Neil would take the same tolerant view. A passing affair didn't attract me. I'd had a few of those since the divorce, and each time I ended feeling bored and at loose ends.

Was there something in between? Why not give it a try? I didn't really want to be involved, to care enough to risk losing my independence. Better wait till he arrived and see how things go.

Neil hadn't been there an hour before I knew I wanted him around in my life one way or another. Never mind the analysis.

When he had checked out my bruises and bumps, with much clucking, I produced the take-away I'd brought in from the local Tandoori. I hoped his wife hadn't been a gourmet cook, because I'd never compete in that department.

Over the food and a bottle of pretty good Verdicchio, I had my first view of the around-the-house Neil. In jeans and a sweater, worry over the Darla Brown case put aside for the moment, he was an easy companion. I had seen all his sterling qualities. Now I realized he was simply fun to be with.

I filled him in on my encounter with Harriet Thorne at the Hayward Gallery. "What doesn't make sense is what she was so afraid of. If she wants to avoid her grandmother, I could see she might be annoyed at some strange lady interfering in her life, but the minute I said her name, she turned and stared at me, and she was terrified. There was no mistaking that."

Neil pondered. "She's obviously in some kind of trouble. She moved out of her digs and left her job. Where was she working?"

"That's the problem. We don't know. Evidently her grandmother doesn't take much interest in details. She told Bea the girl was a shop assistant, but what kind of shop or where it was didn't seem to be on her need-to-know list. Whatever is wrong with Harriet, I'll tell you this: the boyfriend knows all about it, because he definitely tried to stop me from following her. He blocked the doorway to cut me off, but he couldn't very well hold me by force without causing a scene."

We finally gave up on Harriet, and Neil asked how things were going with Mary Louise Talbot. I reported some of my thoughts on *The Specimen* and he said, "That's the first Talbot novel I read, long ago. I don't imagine I regarded myself as a defender of women's rights in those days, but I remember thinking that autocratic fathers were an abomination. Still are, I should think."

"There are plenty of them around, of course. Human nature doesn't change that much. The difference today is that social attitudes would give Emily more support for asserting herself. She was pretty helpless out there on the end of a plank. Either give in to Papa or jump."

"Right. He might not have sent her off to a nunnery but one can guess that he would make her life intolerable, poor girl."

I asked how the case was going and got a shrug. "We've got HOLMES working on possible sources for the cyanide, not only in Devon but around the country. My officers are checking out every lead, but no luck so far. Nothing new on Darla Brown, needless to say."

"Is HOLMES really helpful?"

"It's excellent for gathering information and processing it quickly. It can't do the thinking, of course. We still need people for that."

Originally, I remembered, the acronym for the computer system that had been in use by the police since the 1970s had been simply HOMES, for Home Office Major Enquiry System, until some wag decided that Sherlock should be recognized and had the "L" inserted, with the awkward but amusing result of "Large Major Enquiries System."

Neil added, "We're in luck in one respect. Our system in Devon and Cornwall is compatible with the one here in London."

"Aren't they all the same?"

"No. As each constabulary began to use computers, the chief constable selected the brand he wanted, so we have several different systems scattered around the U.K. Actually, HOLMES follows the old hand-written card system, but when the information is entered, the machines can do some valuable cross-checks at a speed that was impossible before."

"Do you list each case under the name of the victim—such as the 'Darla Brown' file?"

"No, quite the contrary. For security reasons, we use a code name that is as unconnected as possible from the crime itself."

"So if I'd been murdered on the bridge last night, you wouldn't file it under 'Claire'?"

"No." Neil reached over and felt again for the bump on the back of my head. "Good job it was no worse than this, love. I'd rather not have you in a murder file."

After dinner, as we sat on the sofa with our coffee, Neil said, "I'm glad we had that dinner in Torquay, Claire."

I smiled. "Why?"

"It was about halfway through the meal that you woke up and looked at me for the first time as if I were something more than a piece of furniture."

Remembering, I said, "Was it that obvious?"

"It was."

I looked at the upward curve of his mouth and the amusement in his dark eyes and knew I was hooked.

As we drifted toward the bedroom, Neil said, "I had to leave your number with my sergeant. I hope you don't mind."

I laughed. "Not if he doesn't ring in the next hour."

It was, in fact, a little more than an hour later when the sergeant did ring. As we lay dozing, I answered the bedside phone and handed it to Neil, who listened to the officer's report and than said, with a wink at me, "I'll be stopping over with friends at this number, sergeant. See you in the morning."

We snuggled for a bit. Then I asked, "The sergeant had no news, I gather?"

"No, nothing important. They're checking out a lead on the cyanide but it can wait until morning."

Later on, we decided on some midnight coffee and I brought our cups out by the sofa. Curled up against Neil, I felt it was time to talk about my marriage. "You do know about Miles, I suppose?"

There was a pause. "Yes. I see him occasionally at the Home Office. Is he still with the same—er—person?"

"Yes. Pierre is really quite charming. Sally likes him too, which is good."

"Then she visits her father?"

"Oh, yes, they adore each other. She was seventeen when the break came, old enough to understand the unconventional nature of the arrangement but mature enough to handle it. If it had happened in the States, it would have been much more difficult, I think. The tolerance level is not high in our Puritan society."

"Did you have any idea—?"

"No, none. Miles told me that from adolescence he had felt drawn toward his own sex, but in spite of all we hear about English boys' schools, he had no sexual experiences at that age, not even fooling about. His upbringing was so conventional, his parents so affectionate, that he simply followed the expected path. Besides, he genuinely liked girls too. It seems there is a spectrum of inclinations, as with all things in life, and he was rather close to the center."

Neil said, "Like handedness."

"Like what—?"

"You know, decidedly left-handed to decidedly right-handed, and all those gradations in between, including the rare persons who are almost equally ambidextrous."

I laughed. "Exactly! I think that may be why I was able to understand Miles's dilemma as well as I do. I knew that he had really cared for me and grieved over hurting me. The pain I felt was simply for losing him. For his mother, of course, it's different. She feels what he is doing is morally wrong, and I'm sure his father would have agreed. In fact, it was within the year after his father died that Miles finally made the break. I think he couldn't have done it before."

"You're on good terms, then?"

"Oh, yes, we are now. At first it was uphill for me, but because of Sally we must keep in touch, and it gets easier with time. At the moment, they are in Normandy on holiday, where Pierre's family has a summer place, but I'll see them when they come back to London."

I got up to pour more coffee, and in the kitchen I leaned against the counter, feeling an irrational surge of relief. It oughtn't to have mattered to me if Neil Padgett had disapproved of Miles's lifestyle, but somehow it did matter. His casual acceptance made me feel closer to him, more willing to make him a part of my life.

We slept in and had a leisurely breakfast. Surprised that Neil didn't have to dash off at the crack of dawn, I finally heard him say with a yawn, "I expect I should turn up by half-past nine or so and act as if I had some official reason to be here."

"You mean you don't?"

"No, darling. There's nothing here in London any of my officers couldn't do. I simply announced I was coming up to London and left my DCI in charge. He looked at me rather oddly but said nothing."

I laughed. "A detective chief inspector does not question the ways of a detective superintendent?"

"Precisely. Now, how soon can you come down to Devon?"

"Hmmm. Since I made such a fuss about getting back to my work, Bea and Sally will certainly think it's strange if I turn up again. Oh, I have it! Sally asked me to go to the annual party of the Letterbox Society on Sunday. I can go down for that."

Neil paused. "Any chance of staying over at my place?"

I thought that one over for about ten seconds. "Yes, why not? I'll just tell Bea the truth. I'm too old to hide things from my mother-in-law."

I repressed a grin, thinking that I'd never have to conceal my amours from my own mother. Known as the Bolter, straight out of Nancy Mitford, my feckless and utterly winsome mother was in her fourth marriage, each of the last three husbands richer than the one before, which was handy for me, as she often sent me her cast-off designer clothes. Sooner or later, I would tell Neil that saga, but I decided it could wait.

That evening, back at his place in Devon, Neil rang up. After some cosy chitchat, we moved on to the murder case. It seems there had been one glimmer of a lead on the cyanide. About five weeks ago a van belonging to a chemical company had been stolen outside a veterinarian's office in north London, where the driver was making a delivery. Against all regulations, he had left the motor running while he dashed inside, and some enterprising thief had simply driven off.

The theft of the van was commonplace enough, but it caused a stir because among the chemicals it carried was a tin of sodium cyanide. The news media gave the story a big play to warn the unwary of the danger of leaving the stuff lying about where children or animals might get hold of it. The powder is harmless enough when dry, but when combined with liquid or moisture it becomes deadly.

Now there was a lead on the theft of the van. A woman who had been badly beaten by her boyfriend had babbled in the emergency room about what a scoundrel he was, "always nicking somebody's wallet or painting over stolen cars." Groggy from painkillers, she mumbled about telling him to get rid of that poison in the van. But when the police asked her to name the man, she refused. "He'd kill me, see. He's been sent down once and he don't want to go inside again." After her mind had cleared, she denied everything and refused to say another word.

"It's not much to go on," Neil said on the phone, "but the connection between 'poison' and 'van' leaped out at us. The London chaps will try to keep an eye out in case the man visits his lady again."

And we said an affectionate good-night.

12

THE NEXT MORNING I TELEPHONED SALLY TO CONFIRM that I would come down to Devon on the weekend for the Letterbox party, then rang Bea to tell her I would see her on Sunday but that I would not be staying with her, as a friend had asked me to his place for the night.

Bea didn't sound all that surprised. "Is it that nice Superintendent Padgett?"

"Yes, it is."

"That's lovely, dear."

I smiled. Was it only a week ago I had firmly resolved to keep men out of my life? Oh, well.

Back at my desk, I picked up my well-thumbed copy of *The Specimen.* In the evening of the day in which Sir Wilfred had given Emily the ring, and she had run to Annette in her distress, Annette confided to her cousin that John Travis, the steward on the estate, had asked her to marry him:

> *'Oh, Annette, he's such a fine man. Will you accept?'*
> *'I don't know, Emily. I like him but I cannot say that*

I love him.' Annette's eyes looked wearily at the ring on Emily's hand. 'Shall we have two loveless marriages? It would be fitting, would it not?'

Emily's eyes filled with tears. 'Why must we marry at all? If only we could go on just as we are. But Annette, if you became Johnny Travis's stepmother, you could do wonders with the boy.'

'I'm not so sure. He likes me well enough now, but if I became his father's wife, I would be a symbol of authority to him, the very thing against which he rebels so violently.'

'Yes, I see.'

Looking with pity at her cousin's pale face, Emily bent forward and kissed her. 'Try to rest now.'

Stephen Ward had returned to Hazelwood, reporting that his mother's health was much improved. When he saw the ring on Emily's finger, his eyes had looked into hers and seen sorrow, not the joy of a young woman engaged to be married. Seeking out Annette, he had learned the full story. Now he gathered his courage to speak of it to Emily.

As Emily sat at the piano and began to play the opening bars of a song, Stephen stood looking down at her and placed his hand over the music.

'I have something to say to you, Miss Spalding, which I much regret.'

Emily looked up at the dearly-loved face, the softly waving hair on his forehead, the fine sensitivity of his lips. 'Yes, Mr. Ward?'

'I believe you are engaged to be married to Sir Wilfred Probis?'

'It is not quite certain, as I believe my cousin Annette has told you.'

'Yes.'

'My father wishes it, you see.'

'I understand. I wish with all my heart, Miss Spalding, that circumstances made it possible for me to—to—' Stephen's voice broke, and he added in a whisper, *'To alter the course of events.'*

Emily looked into his eyes, and all the love of her young heart was there before him.

Thrusting back the anguish that threatened to engulf him, Stephen spoke in a firmer voice. 'As that cannot be, my dear Miss Spalding, I believe it is best for me to tender my resignation to your father. You will understand that it is not possible for me to continue here as your instructor.'

In a quick movement, Emily put out her hand to him and Stephen took it in both of his own. For a long moment, their eyes held. Then Emily ran from the room, the tears she had held back pouring freely down her cheeks.

All this was a pretty standard Victorian love scene, but it seemed to me that apart from the rather stilted language, there was a stir of genuine emotion. Sentimental? Sure, but lovers are still that way, they merely use a different vocabulary. It's the theme of self-sacrifice that dates the novel more than its language. In the latter years of the twentieth century, we don't go in heavily for self-sacrifice. The thrust of our society is toward getting—more money, more sex, more of whatever you want. The flip side is that the individual has more choice. When the options are open, there is less sense of oppression. Decisions taken may be wrong, but at least they are available.

The next morning after Stephen Ward's announcement that he would leave Hazelwood, Emily Spalding looked out the window of her boudoir and saw her cousin Annette strolling in the garden with Sir

Wilfred Probis. At one point, they stopped and faced each other, speaking earnestly. Then Sir Wilfred nodded and gave the young woman a reassuring pat on the shoulder. Feeling qualms of guilt, Emily turned away from the window, saying to herself, "He *is* a kind man, after all. I'm sure Papa wants only what is best for me." And she resolved that, as soon as Stephen Ward had gone, she would sincerely try to grow fond of Sir Wilfred.

That afternoon, when Sir Wilfred came for tea, Talbot gives us a view of Mr. Spalding in all his tactless glory:

After his second slice of cake, George Spalding leaned back in his chair, adjusting his stout body to its contours, and smiled with satisfaction.

'Now then, Miss Annette.'

Startled, Annette looked up at her uncle. He rarely spoke to her except to ask her for more tea or to ring for a servant.

'Travis has been to see me. It seems he wants to make you an offer. Has he spoken to you as yet?'

Annette flinched, and a tide of color flooded her neck and spread upward to her face. It had not occurred to George Spalding that the young woman might not wish to have her innermost feelings discussed at the tea table.

Emily cried out 'Papa!' but her protest was ignored. 'So what do you say, eh?'

Annette looked despairingly at Emily, then turned her eyes to Sir Wilfred.

With a kindly smile, Sir Wilfred said, 'A splendid fellow, Travis.'

Annette was silent as the color ebbed from her face, leaving a pallor more intense than before. Then she looked at the two men and spoke with a bitterness that wrung Emily's heart. 'Yes, Mr. Travis is a good man. As a penniless beggar, I should be grateful for any offer that comes my way. Now, if you will excuse me. . . .' And she rose with dignity and left the room.

George Spalding nodded approvingly. 'Yes, indeed, she's quite right, you know. Can't be many chaps who would take the girl without a penny. I'll give them a handsome gift when the time comes.'

It was the next day that the tragedy occurred. Stephen Ward had decided to leave before the end of his week's notice, and this was to be his last day at Hazelwood. Restless and unable to sleep, Emily had risen early and gone for a walk in the grounds. Her thoughts preoccupied with Stephen's departure, she followed a path through a copse of beech trees, skirted the lake, and went deeper into the wood on the far side, where a little stream that fed the lake marked the line between her father's property and that of Sir Wilfred:

Cool at this hour, the day yet gave the promise of late-summer sunshine. The dew on the open lawns was already drying, while here under the trees it still clung to shrub and leaf. Stephen's last day—and then they would never meet again. Her father had accepted Stephen's resignation with complete indifference.

'Well, well, a pleasant enough young person,' he had said to Emily. 'Shall I engage someone else to take his place?'

When she demurred, her father had seemed relieved not to be troubled further and had said no more about it.

Her head bent, Emily walked swiftly along the path when a glimmer of something white caught her eye. On the other side of a tree, some distance from the path, she saw what looked to be a bit of white cloth near the foot of the tree. Curious, she turned and walked through the sparse fern toward a small clearing ahead. As she came closer, the white cloth took shape. An arm, in a white sleeve? Was someone sitting at the foot of the tree, facing into the clearing?

Closer yet, she saw the lace at the edge of the sleeve. A woman!

'Hello!' she called out.

No answer.

Approaching cautiously, Emily circled a large oak and stepped into the clearing. And then she stopped and gazed in horror. A woman was sitting at the base of the tree, her head hanging forward, her dark hair loosened and covering her face. The shaft of an arrow protruded from the woman's chest, and a reddish streak ran down the white dress.

Leaping forward, Emily pushed the hair away from the woman's face and recoiled in anguish. 'Annette! Oh, my darling!'

Grasping the arrow with both hands, she tugged until it came free and caught her cousin's body as it toppled forward, placing her on her back on the ground. The first wild hope that Annette might still be alive now faded. The flesh of the arms, bare below the elbow, was ominously cold, and Emily's frantic efforts to arouse her cousin failed utterly.

Still, she could not be certain. If a doctor came soon enough, Annette might still be saved.

Running with desperate haste, Emily went back along the path, stopping now and then to catch her breath, then pressing on until a pain in her side forced her to slow her pace. As at last she reached the terrace of the house, she saw Stephen Ward coming toward her.

Without a moment's hesitation, she threw herself into his arms. 'Oh, Stephen!' she sobbed, using for the

first time the name that was always in her thoughts.
'It's Annette! We must send for a doctor!'

Holding her close to his heart, he murmured, 'It's all
right, my darling. Tell me what happened.'

When she had choked out her story, Stephen moved
quickly. Putting Emily into a chair, he ran into the
house, stopping the first servant he encountered to
rouse George Spalding from his bed, while another was
dispatched to the village for the doctor.

But the doctor, when he came, could do nothing. He
pronounced that the girl had been dead for more than
an hour. The local police, unprepared to handle a case
of murder among the gentry, called in Scotland Yard,
and thus the character of Inspector Vickers was
introduced to Victorian fiction.

One of the aspects of Talbot's writing that I planned
to deal with in the biography was that, in common
with fellow "sensation" novelists, she anticipated
many features of the mystery novel as it eventually
took form in the twentieth century. Not only does *The*
Specimen contain the elements of a whodunit plot, it
also introduces a policeman as dedicated as Dickens's
Inspector Bucket in *Bleak House* and has the distinc-
tion of preceding by several years the appearance of
Wilkie Collins's celebrated Sergeant Cuff in *The*
Moonstone.

A thin man with a sharp nose and piercing eyes,
Inspector Vickers questioned the members of the
Hazelwood household and the staff from the butler to
the stable boy. He soon saw that the obvious suspect
was young Johnny Travis. In a long interview with the
boy, who was in tears and obviously devastated by the
death of Annette, Vickers tried to prod him into
admitting that the shooting of the fatal arrow was an
accident, that the boy may even have been unaware of

the result of a random shot, but Johnny persisted in his story that he was asleep and was awakened by the sound of voices below the loft where he slept. He heard them talking of finding Annette's body and ran down to learn of the tragedy.

George Spalding sputtered with fury when Vickers failed to arrest Johnny at once. "Any fool can see the boy did it, Inspector. How else could it have happened, I ask you that?"

Vickers merely nodded. "That is what I am here to determine, sir."

And with that George Spalding had to be content.

13

By Sunday morning, in spite of the usual interruptions and some pleasant intervals renewing London friendships, I had managed to get a good swatch of work done on the book and set off for Devon in a pleasant euphoria. Bea had talked me into staying on Monday night with her, as she wanted to take me to a special dinner somewhere out on the moor. The plan was that I would stop first at Bea's, where our Letterbox group would gather, taking my car to Princetown and going on to Neil's place in Kings Abbey later in the evening. The extra day with Bea wouldn't hurt me, I decided. I'd earned some time off.

Bea hugged me with special warmth. "Claire, dear, I'm so pleased. I quite like your Mr. Padgett!"

I wondered if Bea had adopted a more liberal view than I would have expected toward extramarital sex. On the other hand, the darling was quite capable of believing that when I stayed over with Neil, he would sleep on the sofa, and I wasn't about to disillusion her. In any case, I was glad she was happy.

We chatted about this and that, and when I asked after Mabel Thorne, Bea looked troubled. She had told me on the phone that Harriet had indeed phoned her grandmother on the day after I saw her at the Hayward Gallery. Now Bea said, "Mabel was relieved to hear from Harriet, thanks to your efforts, Claire, but she's puzzled that Harriet still wouldn't give her even a temporary address. At least, the girl promised to ring again in a week's time."

"Good. How is Mabel's health?"

"I'm afraid she's no better. It was only on Monday that you so kindly took her in to the doctor, and she's been reclining on the sofa almost ever since. I've tried to ask her what the doctor said, but she brushes it off and insists it's nothing serious."

"She looked pretty ill to me."

"Exactly. She's most grateful to you, Claire, and asked me to thank you again for your efforts. She'll write you a note when she's better."

I knew it was no good saying never mind the note. If Mabel's rigid sense of propriety required a note, a note I would get. It was a gauge of how ill she was that she was unable to perform even that simple task.

When the phone rang, Bea answered, then broke into a broad smile. "Oh, Stella, that's marvelous! Hang on. Claire's here, I'll tell her." And to me: "Oliver's name is on the short list for selection."

When we had both expressed our pleasure at the news, Bea said, "Stella wants you to come to her place for a sandwich. I'll be leaving for church soon. Shall I say yes?"

"May I take the bicycle?"

"Of course, dear."

I reached for the phone. "Stella! Yes, I'd love it. If I ride Bea's bike, can I come in through the back gate?"

"Of course, darling. Come along. Oliver's out politicking."

"Right."

By half-past eleven, I was pedalling through the outer fringes of Morbridge and along a road that led out onto the moor, where a track would eventually diverge and take me to a farm gate a quarter of a mile below the Bascombs' place. Desperate for exercise after days of sitting at my desk, I felt the sheer physical exuberance of moving through the balmy air of a near-perfect day in early June.

Bea's ten-speed behaved admirably as I sailed up the first long slope, leaving the town behind me. Now the open moor lay before me, thickly green with the low gorse that would blaze with color in another month or so. Curving, the road dropped down, then rose again over the undulating hills. In the hollow, I felt cut off from everything but the rocky soil around me, with its barren patches, but at the next rise, vistas magically appeared, the land at my left dropping away to a valley of greens and browns, while far ahead and to the right, high ridges ringed the horizon.

Presently I passed within a hundred yards or so of an ancient stone cross standing alone in a field, one of many that dotted the moor from Saxon times. I crossed a little stream that meandered along a stony bed, and everywhere were tiny shallow pools that reminded me of the larger pool where Darla Brown's body had been found, some miles beyond.

I had no fear of losing my way, although it had been more than three years since those days when Miles and I used to bicycle together and had sometimes taken this shortcut to visit Oliver and Stella.

When I reached the track that cut across the road, I saw by my watch that I was early and decided to turn left and have a look at the site known as Gray's Quarry. It fascinated me that looking out at the terrain, you could see no hint of anything ahead until you came up to the edge and looked down into a scene that was right out of a child's picture book. Leafy trees with gracefully spread branches lined the steep sides where long ago granite had been cut and hauled away on the down-sloping land of the far side. Water had filled the bottom of the quarry, forming a pond, green with the reflection of the drooping trees.

In the midst of the wild moor, with its stubby vegetation, this Eden-like oasis startled the senses. Unable to resist its lure, I left my bike and walked down the path that led from the rim to the old quarry floor, as I had done in the past. Picking my way through ferns that grew among the rocks, I reached the edge of the pool and put my hand into its cool water.

At a sound behind me, I turned but saw nothing. Probably a small creature rustling in the undergrowth. People did come along occasionally, I knew, but if anyone had scrambled down the path after me, I would have heard more noise. With a shrug, I stood up and looked slowly around, marveling at how huge blocks of stone had been moved without the aid of modern machinery. Still, if men could build the pyramids, this must have been a piece of cake.

Back in the sheer wall to my right I saw the entrance to the cave that nature had formed in the rock face. No time to explore today. Stella was expecting me.

Circling past the cave toward the path, I saw what looked like the rim and tire of a bicycle protruding from under some ferns. Curious, I bent over for a closer look.

"Now then! Be off with you!"

I leaped up at the voice not six feet from my back. Standing at the entrance to the cave was the woman

I'd seen in Morbridge on her bicycle, her gray hair like cactus spikes, her haggard face contorted with anger. Behind her, in the cave, I glimpsed a folding chair and a large box with utensils set out like a tabletop.

"I'm so sorry," I said soothingly. "I had no idea anyone was here."

Now the woman looked into my face. "I've seen you before. You know *her,* don't you now?"

"Who—?"

"Her, that's who. The Bitch!"

"I'm afraid I don't know—"

"Don't deny it. I've seen you." Now she held up a fist and took a menacing step toward me. "And don't tell anyone you've seen me here, or you'll regret it."

"Yes, of course."

"Don't tell *her,* understand?"

"I promise!"

I backed up and literally ran for the path, reaching the top in record time.

Poor creature—she must be slightly mad, I thought, as I pedalled back along the track, recrossed the road, and started up the slope toward the Bascomb place. Who on earth could the woman have seen me with?

Then it occurred to me that all of this land, including the site of the old quarry and many acres beyond it, belonged to Oliver. Technically, the woman was trespassing if, as it appeared, she was living in the cave. Maybe she had done this in the past and Stella had had her removed, thus qualifying as the "bitch." Certainly, she might have seen me with Stella somewhere last weekend.

I resolved to say nothing to Stella in any case. The woman appeared to be doing no harm at the moment. Let the Bascombs deal with her if it became a problem.

As I went through the farm gate, the weather did

one of its notorious flips. The sun dodged behind some innocent-looking clouds, which promptly turned blackish and began pelting me with rain. Coming to a large shed, I propped my bike against its side, snatched my waterproof jacket out of the carrier, and stepped inside the shed while I got into the jacket and zipped it up. The rows of supplies on shelves, the assorted tools and equipment, reminded me that Oliver's place was a working farm, not the amusement of a gentleman. Sheep and crops were serious business in these parts.

I pulled the hood over my head and rode on up the final hill to the house, arriving not more than slightly damp underneath.

Stella took away my dripping jacket and handed me a dry sweater and a sherry. "Darling! This is marvelous! We didn't expect to see you so soon again."

I gave her the line about the Letterbox party and she accepted that. I wasn't ready to talk about Neil yet.

This was definitely one of Stella's tacky days. In jeans and a sweatshirt, her hair hanging loose, her huge black eyes looming over the planes and hollows of her face, she looked more like a gypsy than the lady of the manor.

"Kitchen all right?" she asked.

"Of course."

I loved the big kitchen at Herons, where the scrubbed wood table stood by a bank of windows looking out across the moorland. Now I noticed that Stella's hands were not quite steady as she put out our sandwiches and poured coffee. We munched in silence for a bit. Then I said, tentatively, "Stella?"

She shot me a grateful look. "Yes, darling, trouble. Thank God you're here. I need your advice, and I can't talk to *anyone* hereabouts, you understand."

"Tell me."

"On Thursday, I received a phone call. The voice was disguised with one of those quacking devices— you know what I mean."

"Like Donald Duck?"

"Exactly. But I'm convinced it was a woman. She said she had seen Oliver having a picnic lunch with Darla Brown some months ago."

"When exactly?"

"The middle of February."

I snorted. "A picnic in Devon in *February*? Is she kidding?"

"That's more or less what I said, and she said by 'picnic' she meant they were sitting in the car under the trees up by Becky Falls and were eating sandwiches, and she was sure they were kissing."

"Oh, dear. I see the problem. Even if Oliver was silly enough to take the girl for a drive, he's told everyone he scarcely knew her."

"Exactly. Once a rumor like this begins, it could be blown up and distorted, and it could destroy his chances in the election."

"What does Oliver say?"

Stella waited one beat too long to answer. She looked out at the moor, then turned her eyes to mine. "Oh, he says it's nonsense. The woman must be inventing the whole story."

As her eyes swivelled away again, I said quietly, "But you're not sure you believe him."

Stella's voice was low. "Oliver's terribly susceptible where women are concerned. They throw themselves at his head and of course he's flattered. One can't blame him for that. Now and then he fails to resist temptation and gets involved in flirtations."

"I see." I didn't doubt that for a moment. I was more surprised that gorgeous Oliver would stoop to wasting his talents on Darla Brown until I remembered the snapshots of sexy Darla in Harriet Thorne's album. If those two were parked under the trees, I'd be willing to bet it didn't stop at flirtation.

"So, Stella, why is this woman calling you now?"

"I think you can guess. She wants money."

"Oh, Lord. You can't pay her, you know. If you do, she'll have proof you believe her story."

"I've thought of that. But Claire, if I can keep her from going to the newspapers, don't you see it would be worth it?"

"Does Oliver think you should pay?"

The huge eyes stared into mine. "I didn't tell him that part of it."

"My God, Stella, why not?"

"I can't have him worried, don't you see? I'll handle this myself."

We chewed that one over for a while, but I didn't have much luck getting Stella to change her mind. The woman was due to telephone again on Monday, presumably while Oliver was at his office.

"You see, Claire," she said, "we've waited too long for this. I can't let anything stand in the way now that Oliver's chance has come. If I do pay, I shall make absolutely certain nothing can be traced to me. It would be my word against hers. So you see how vital it is to say nothing about this to anyone!"

I promised. I noticed that people who ask for advice rarely take it, but at least I was sure Stella felt better for having talked it out.

By two o'clock, the rain had ceased as abruptly as it had begun, and I pedalled back from Herons to Bea's place through benign sunshine. I must have been halfway there when something clicked. The woman had claimed she saw Oliver with Darla during the middle of February. Darla was certainly in Morbridge around that time. At the inquest, Mrs. Brown mentioned that her daughter had come home for a visit in February. According to the postmortem, Darla was nine or ten weeks pregnant when she died, which was in late April.

The timing was ominous, as Stella must have been aware. Now I saw why she was so keen to pay off the blackmailer. Even to me, Stella could not express her deepest fear—that Oliver might be the father of Darla Brown's unborn child.

DARTMOOR BURIAL

14

I GOT TO BEA'S IN TIME TO SHOWER AND CHANGE. SALLY arrived with Jason, followed by William Trask, who brought two friends along, sturdy young men who looked as if they could stride the moors with the best of them. He also brought Ruby Brown, Darla's sister. "Poor kid," Jason had said to Sally, "she doesn't get many good times."

Sally, who never hesitated to manage things, announced that she and Ruby and Jason would ride over with me, and they could all squeeze up in William's car coming back. Bea, having no desire to sit through hours of dancing in the evening, waved us off with her blessing. Sally climbed into the back seat with Ruby, confirming that Jason, who sat up front with me, was "just a friend, not a date."

We set off across the moor, taking a road that wound through a patch of woods and then emerged into a landscape so barren it could have been a moonscape except for the vegetation that covered the folded humps of hills. Black-faced sheep picked their way over the rocky soil, nibbling snacks of gorse, and here and there, the granite outcroppings of the tors took on anthropomorphic shapes.

For more than twenty miles, we drove through the hauntingly desolate terrain, passing an occasional farmhouse or a tiny hamlet at a crossroads, when at last, from the crest of a high down, we saw on a distant rise of ground the bleak stone buildings of Her Majesty's Prison at Princetown.

Originally built for prisoners of war in the days of Napoleon, the prison had later been used for criminals convicted of the most serious offenses, but now, I understood, it had been purged of its reputation for grim horror and housed convicts of a wide variety of crimes. Still, I thought, enlightened administration or not, one look at those forbidding portals would not cheer the heart of an arriving prisoner.

Following Jason's directions, I drove through the little town, chiefly occupied by the prison officers and their families, and along the road toward the prison, turning, before reaching those gray stone structures, into a car park beside a low building which proved to be the Social Club.

The party was in full swing when we arrived. The long room, pub-like with its extended bar, red and black carpet, fruit machines, and walls lined with booths and tables, resounded with good cheer. William Trask, who had come in minutes before us, pointed to the table his friends were holding and took our orders, mine for white wine, Sally's and Jason's for lagers, and Ruby Brown saying shyly she'd like a lemon squash.

At fourteen, Ruby was at an awkward age. In the car, she had said very little but seemed to enjoy listening to the rest of us as we chatted on about this and that. Now, when William returned with our drinks, Ruby sat between Jason and me, her thin body shrinking against the back of the booth, her freckled face turned toward the group in silent scrutiny.

There was lots of table-hopping, as people stopped by our table to chat and exchange letterboxing stories, while Jason gave us a running commentary. "These chaps are from Kings Abbey," or "We met these girls last year—they're from over at Yelverton." Several men were identified as prison officers, cheery souls spouting jokes and laughter.

There were snatches of conversation about Darla Brown from those who remembered her from the party the year before. One woman remarked, "Such a pretty girl she was. How tragic to die so young."

One of the officers said, "She seemed very taken with that chap Malone, do you remember?" and his friend replied, "Malone? Yes, that young fellow had an eye for the ladies, all right. Not enough action for him hereabouts. I took him letterboxing now and then, but walking on the moor wasn't his idea of entertainment."

Soon, our group broke up, as the Trasks and their friends began to circulate and their seats were taken by others. Sally, next to Ruby, was surrounded by young people, and I found myself sitting next to a prison officer who was pleased to find an American lady at the party. "We don't see that many Yanks here."

I smiled. "I'm surprised you fellows are so friendly. I'd have thought you might be on the grim side."

"No. People expect that, but it's a job like any other, and we've a jolly lot here. Most of the chaps like a laugh and a bit of fun."

"Do you chat with the prisoners?"

"Oh, yes. No harm in that. Poor devils, they're not going anywhere."

"Does anyone ever escape?"

He laughed. "Everyone asks us that. Once in a long while one gets out, but he's usually picked up double-quick."

Jason had come back to the table, and seeing I was occupied, said to Sally and Ruby, "Come on, girls, let's cruise."

I said, "Of course, go along," but Ruby hung back. "I'll stay here with Mrs. Camden, if you don't mind."

When the officer had gone, I smiled at Ruby. "Go with Sally and Jason if you like, Ruby."

She shook her head. "I don't like meeting all those people."

"I can't say I blame you. You're fourteen, are you?" She nodded.

"When I was your age, I hated it too."

"You did?"

"Yes. By the time I was sixteen, I got over being shy and the whole world changed."

"Darla was never shy. Mum says I'm stupid and why can't I be more like Darla."

Oh, dear. As there was no comfort I could offer to that one, I said nothing, but Ruby didn't seem to mind.

"Mum carries on about Darla now, but she wasn't all that fond of her when she was alive. Besides, she and me dad are such liars."

I refrained from asking her to go on, but I gave a sympathetic "Mmm" which seemed to suffice.

"At that sort of trial—"

"The inquest?"

"Right, the inquest. Mum said she noticed Darla's clothes on the telly, but she didn't. I was the one as said, 'That looks like Darla's blouse,' and Mum says, 'Don't be silly, Ruby.' Then she looks again and says, 'Oh, it does a bit.' And then she rang up the police.

She never took no notice of Darla after she went off to London."

"But Darla did come back to visit, didn't she?"

"Only to see her friends. She and Mum didn't say much to each other."

"And your father?"

"Darla hated him even more. For a long time she was his favorite, but then they had a falling out and hardly spoke to each other. She only came back to Morbridge when he was gone. He drives a lorry and sometimes he's away for days."

"I see."

"Dad's a liar, too. He said he was home when Darla cut herself with the razor that time, but I know he wasn't. He was gone that day. Darla told me about it when I came home from school and showed me the cut. So why did he say he was there?"

"Have you told the police that?"

"Why would I do that? Dad would only say I was wrong and then he'd take a strap to me. No thanks."

I said quietly, "I'm sorry about what happened to Darla, Ruby."

The sharp little face turned toward me. "It's okay. She never talked to me a whole lot, and we used to have rows because we had to share the bedroom. I liked it when she went to London because I got the room to myself. But still, I wish she hadn't died."

Seeing compassion in my face, she gave me a grateful look and her voice was wistful as she went on. "Last time Darla was home she said there was something she wanted to talk to me about. Then she looked at me and sort of laughed and said, 'I expect it can wait.' Now I'll never know what it was."

"I'm glad you could come today, Ruby."

A radiant smile lit her face. "Oh, yes! Jason's been

that good to me. Sometimes he takes me to a film or for an ice cream. I know it's because he wants to talk about Darla, but I like it anyhow."

As the afternoon went on, and our groups reformed, we heard animated stories of people finding letterboxes or failing to find ones that ought to have been where the guide said they were, or falling into bogs, or being caught out in the sudden mists that came and went alarmingly on the moor with no warning. I learned that a newcomer had to find his or her first hundred letterboxes, usually in the company of a member, before joining and receiving the white "100 Club" badge, which could be sewn on the rucksack. Many friends were congratulated on reaching a new level of achievement: a blue badge for 200, yellow for 500, a special gold one with laurel leaves for 1,000, and so on. Jason, under his brother's tutelage, had already earned his first one hundred and was eager to add to his total when the long vacation began in July.

I said, "There must be thousands of boxes, then, all over Dartmoor?" but someone laughed and explained they're not all there at once, that they come and go and are often changed after a few months. There are also many walks for charity throughout the year, where the walker pays his contribution to obtain the clue sheet, and the boxes are not left out permanently.

Sally said, "Sounds like our walks for good causes, at home in the States, except that you people also get the fun of finding the boxes!"

By six o'clock, Sally and I wandered into a large adjoining room where there were lavish spreads of food. While she heaped her plate, I took bits of this and that, saving room for a proper meal with Neil later on. Jason had taken charge of Ruby for the moment, and we settled into a corner with a couple of glasses of wine.

"Poor old Jason." Sally chewed a barbecued chicken wing, then went on. "He's feeling down because it was just a year ago that Darla let him bring her to this party. I told him he could tell his troubles to Aunt Sally, and he did."

Between bites, Sally gave me Jason's story. "He was pretty excited when she agreed to come with him, but it didn't last long. They drove over with William and another guy, and it seems Darla flirted with William on the way over and pretty much ignored Jason. I guess William tried to be decent about it, but he was flattered and didn't exactly push her away. Jason was eighteen then and William was twenty-two. When Darla insisted on dancing a lot with William, he did make her dance with Jason once or twice, but it didn't do much good.

"Then, just when it looked as if William was about to be crowned Prince Consort, Darla met up with a prison officer, some guy named Malone, and the Trask boys were dumped in a hurry. She spent the rest of the evening with Malone, and as a final insult, said a casual thanks to the brothers and let Malone take her home. Jason says William never mentioned her name again, and he was pretty shaken up when he found out it was Darla's body he found in the bog. Poor old Jason still carries the torch, probably because it was his first love and nobody's come along to make him forget."

I said, "Jason strikes me as a classic case of the late bloomer. In a year or two, he may turn out to be an attractive young man."

Sally pondered. "Could be. Hard to say."

"I wonder if the man Malone is here at the party?"

"No. Jason says he asked after him and found out

he had left his job here several months ago, one officer thought around October of last year."

"Hmm. That's about the time Darla went to London, isn't it? I wonder."

"It's possible. Jason asked Ruby if Darla ever mentioned Malone and she says, not to her. But there was one thing: Last summer Darla did talk about Princetown Prison to Ruby a few times. Maybe this Malone was married, and that's why she didn't mention his name."

"Well, if that's the case, he couldn't be the mysterious fiancé in London, could he?"

Sally sighed. "Unless he got divorced. But in that case, why all the secrecy?"

By half-past six, I said goodbye to Sally and her friends and set off on a road that would take me directly to Kings Abbey, passing in the last few miles through a lush countryside of wooded forest and rushing streams as different as one could imagine from the barren moorland that surrounded the prison.

Being with Neil was already natural and easy. We seemed to feel a sense of belonging together that was both exhilarating and comforting.

Over drinks, he asked if I wanted to go out for a meal or stay in and have Chinese take-away. I looked around at his comfortable flat, with its walls of books, and smiled into his eyes. "I like it here," I said.

Curled up on the sofa, we talked about this and that. When I remarked that I couldn't understand why it had taken me so long to see what a gem he was, he said it wasn't all that surprising. "When we met last summer in London, I was still pretty depressed over the breakup of my marriage, and I probably came over as Mr. Grimsby."

I laughed. "And I was no doubt Ms. Prickly. I had

just disentangled myself from a relationship that was driving me up the wall, and I wasn't looking for another one.''

Sooner or later, we got around to talking about the Darla Brown case. Neil said there had been what might be a new development, although the connection was pretty tenuous. It seems the London police had located a chap named Hopkins who had probably painted the stolen van, the one with the tin of cyanide in the back.

I said, "Did they keep a watch on the lady friend's house, then?"

"No, they got a tipoff from a disgruntled neighbor. The man next door had been fed up with the goings-on in the garage—noise and confusion, and cars coming in and out at all hours of the night, and he promised to call in if Hopkins turned up. The call came late yesterday, and they nipped out and brought him in for questioning. He admitted to painting cars "for friends" now and then. When told that witnesses had seen the van there several weeks ago, he admitted to painting a van around that time—dark blue over white—but claimed there had been no lettering on it when it came in.''

"What about the cyanide?"

"He said his lady friend went on about some kind of poison but he 'never saw nothin' like that' and implied she was off her rocker. As for the owner of the van, needless to say he was sent by a friend and Hopkins never knew the man's name nor where the van is now.''

"A likely story, I'm sure."

"Exactly. The significant news is that Hopkins has been in and out of prison on counts from petty theft to burglary. His last sojourn as a guest of Her Majesty was two years and a half at—guess where? None other than Princetown. He was released last September and came up to London. Claims he's been straight ever since. I've sent a man up to see if he can find any connection with Darla Brown. It's the only lead we have, and we're going to give it the full treatment."

"I don't suppose Hopkins could be the mysterious fiancé?"

"I'd like to think so, but he's forty-eight years old and an ugly little weasel. Granting there's no accounting for tastes, it's hard to believe our Darla would fancy him."

I said, "Speaking of Princetown, little Ruby Brown gave me an earful this afternoon." And I told Neil the substance of our conversation.

He frowned. "Sounds as if Darla really hated her parents, beyond the usual teen rebellion. Especially the father."

"Yes. If Ruby spoke of the father taking a strap to her, it seems likely he did the same to Darla. And it looks as if the mother did nothing to defend her daughter. I'm afraid that's a pattern that's all too common. The girl leaves home the minute she can get away. Darla did well to hang in till she finished her O levels."

"Yes, poor child. What puzzles me is this: If Darla came back to Morbridge only to visit her friends, not to see her family, the question is, what friends? With all our investigation, we haven't been able to locate anybody who saw much of her on those two visits."

I had told Neil earlier of hearing the chat between the pregnant woman and the receptionist in the office of Mabel Thorne's doctor, suggesting that Darla had a date for lunch with someone that day in April, but the police had never learned who it was.

Now I faced up to my own dilemma. I knew that theoretically I should tell Neil about the claim of the blackmailer that Oliver Bascomb had been seen with Darla in February, but I simply couldn't do it. Stella trusted me utterly, and a rumor of this kind could destroy Oliver's political future. It was impossible that either Oliver or Stella could have any connection with Darla's murder, and after all, how did I know that the accusation was true? Anyone could invent such a story, now that the girl was dead, and try to collect on it, even if there wasn't a shred of truth in it.

Neil's next remark put Oliver and Stella out of my mind. "In a few days, my sweet, I suspect I'll find it necessary to run up to London and question our van-painter in person. How about a room in Bedford Square?"

I snuggled a little closer. "Sounds good to me."

15

THE NEXT MORNING, NEIL HAD ARRANGED NOT TO TURN UP in his office till the afternoon. We had a leisurely breakfast and were lolling around reading the *Guardian* and the local paper like an old married couple when the phone rang.

"Hell and damnation," he said mildly, as he put down the receiver. "The CC is coming along in half an hour and evidently intends to spend the day. I'll have to be there."

The Chief Constable of Devon and Cornwall was Neil's immediate superior, whose presence was a command performance.

I blew him a kiss. "Duty, as Alfred Lord T. was wont to say, is the path to glory."

I rang Bea to say I'd be coming early, and drove into Morbridge, stopping in the town center to see if I could find a ribbon for my word processor, to save myself an extra errand at home. To my surprise, the local stationer had a complete line of equipment and supplies, shaming me into recognizing that Morbridge was not after all living in the Dark Ages.

As I walked back to my car, I came to the office where Oliver Bascomb and his partner practiced law. On an impulse, I walked up the stairs and into the reception room, where I was told by the young lady at the desk that Mr. Bascomb was on the telephone but would be free shortly. I gave her my name and took a chair opposite a door labelled "Oliver Douglas Bascomb."

Might as well wait, I thought. I wanted to ask Oliver a question that was, strictly speaking, not legit, but I figured that as an old friend I could get by with it. He could easily refuse to answer.

Behind the pretty, dark-haired young receptionist, whose desk was in the open area, I could see a balding man working away in a glass-enclosed cubicle, surrounded by legal documents. A male clerk, I thought, like something out of Dickens, except that this one had a word processor instead of a quill pen.

A name-plate on the young woman's desk said "Betty Drake." I smiled at her. "Lovely day, isn't it, Betty?" and got an answering smile and a "Yes, indeed," as she looked out the window at the gleaming sunshine.

I knew the police had questioned her about Darla and learned nothing, but I thought it wouldn't do any harm to have another shot. I said, "I don't believe you were here last year, when I came into the office one day with Mrs. Bascomb?"

The bland smile faded and her dark eyes gave me a sharp look. "No, that is correct. I came here in October last."

"I see. Then you must have taken the post when Darla Brown left?"

"Yes, I did."

Betty picked up a card file and made a show of studying its contents with great concentration, although a moment before she had seemed to have little to do. She hadn't actually been painting her nails or reading a magazine, but she certainly hadn't look overburdened with work.

Ignoring her ploy, I asked, "Did you know Darla, then?"

Reluctantly, she raised her eyes. "Yes, of course." Her tone implied that everyone in a town the size of Morbridge knew everyone else.

"Her death was a tragedy, wasn't it?"

"Certainly." No quiver of sorrow, I noticed.

The telephone emitted a discreet little double buzz, and she picked it up with obvious relief, making an appointment for a client. Then, with a glance at the phone bank, she pressed a button, saying, "Mr. Bascomb, Mrs. Claire Camden is here to see you."

Oliver came bounding out of his office and gave me a warm embrace. "Claire, darling! What a lovely surprise! Come in, come in."

I saw a rosy flush light Betty's face as Oliver came in. Then, as I turned to follow him, I caught a look of sheer animosity directed toward me.

Oh, dear, I thought. Another victim of Oliver's devastating charm.

Oliver's office was decidedly in the tradition of the old-school solicitor, that is to say, it was designed to avoid the appearance of an office and to look instead like a room in a private home. Dark panelled walls with a couple of Constable-like landscapes, deep chairs, exquisite tables and bric-a-brac that had probably been in the Bascomb family for eons, and in the corner, a small rosewood desk discreetly lurking beside an Oriental screen.

Oliver produced the inevitable glass of sherry and

we settled down on a silk-striped sofa to a spate of small talk. I had no problem feeling at ease with him, as I knew he had no idea Stella had told me about the phone call accusing him of hanky-panky with Darla Brown.

When we had covered the weather and I had congratulated him on making the short list for selection, I gave him a slightly diffident smile. "Look, Oliver, I have a truly impertinent question for you, and I expect you not to answer, so do feel free to look inscrutable and usher me out."

He reached over and squeezed my hand. "Yes, darling, what is it?"

"I believe Bea's neighbor, Mrs. Mabel Thorne, is your client. She's been ill, and Bea's wondering if she might need any financial help if things get worse. She can hardly ask Mrs. Thorne herself, as you can imagine, nor would she ask you. I know you can't divulge the status of your clients, but can you give me any sort of hint as to whether this might be a problem?"

Oliver's mouth twitched, then widened into a delighted grin. "Bea is such a dear, isn't she? And it's good of you to ask. Of course I can't officially answer your question, but I believe I can safely say to you that if Mabel Thorne has any problems, the one you suggest is very, *very* far from the mark. You have my permission to relay this to Bea in strictest confidence!"

After some more chitchat, I thanked him and went out, giving Betty an angelic smile as I passed. I longed to pat her on the head and suggest that she stick to her own age group, but it was her problem, not mine.

Bea was glad to hear my report about Mabel. From Oliver's amusement at my question, it was clear she was very well off indeed.

Bea said, "It's so difficult to guess about such things. Mabel does give generously to the church, but she lives otherwise so frugally that I did wonder. And when Harriet went off to London and was working in a shop, there was no hint that Mabel was giving her any help, although the girl must have been on fairly short rations."

Stingy old bat, I thought to myself, now that I knew Mabel was undoubtedly Madam Moneybags.

After lunch, I took out my copy of *The Specimen* to make some notes. I rarely did any actual writing away from my desk, but at this point I needed to reread the section I was working on and select specific passages for commentary.

The character of Inspector Vickers as the incorruptible police officer was not the cliché it might seem to readers today. In 1863, when Mary Louise Talbot was writing the novel, there was still plenty of controversy about how criminals should be detected and brought to justice. In the bad old days of the eighteenth century, much of the work was done by bounty hunters, who sometimes did a good job of hunting down the guilty but who were not always averse to grabbing an innocent suspect in order to get the award money. In the public mind, the spies and informers who brought evidence against criminals were often as much despised as the culprits themselves.

It was not until 1829 that Britain had its first official police force, when Robert Peel's "Bobbies" began patrolling the London streets. It was some years later that the first Detective Department was formed, and by keeping a low profile and avoiding corruption, these officers were gradually able to overcome the long-standing prejudice against the investigators of crime.

When Talbot's Inspector Vickers appeared on the

fictional scene, the Criminal Investigation Department, better known as Scotland Yard, had been in existence less than twenty years and was still not universally accepted. Thus, by making Vickers an admirable character, Talbot lined up on the side of the issue taken by Dickens, who had given the power of his support to the original officers of the Detective Department in the 1840s. The enormous success of Talbot's novel then gave another boost to public acceptance of the fledgling police system.

Social barriers, however, were another matter. While Inspector Vickers was a quiet, courteous man, he was not a "gentleman," and George Spalding, Emily's father, was not about to treat him with respect. As a paid employee of the London Metropolitan Police, Vickers was no better than an underling to Spalding, who fumed at not being able to order him about. He had no objection to Vickers questioning the servants, but he balked at being questioned himself.

When Vickers asked him to confirm his whereabouts on the early morning when Annette's body was found, Spalding snapped, "I was in bed. Where else do you suppose I would be?"

Vickers said quietly, "I believe, sir, you were fully dressed when the servant called you to inform you of the tragedy?"

Spalding blinked. "That's as may be. I sometimes go out for an early walk. I refuse to be questioned like a common criminal, sir. Good day to you."

Meanwhile, Emily was devastated by the horror of finding Annette's body and the grief of losing her beloved cousin. Her only comfort was that, when Stephen Ward left the house, he told her that if she wished, he would stay on for a time at the inn in the village. He would meet her at three o'clock each day at the boathouse beside the lake to offer what consolation he might.

Inspector Vickers was also billeted at the inn, where he took a liking to young Stephen and suggested that Stephen's knowledge of the household at Hazelwood might be of some help in the investigation. On the day following Annette's death, the Inspector took Stephen aside:

'I am going to tell you something in confidence, Mr. Ward. We now have evidence that strongly suggests a case of homicide, although I do not wish as yet to make a public statement to that effect. The doctor reports that there were band-like bruises on the victim's upper arms, under the sleeves of her dress, indicating that she had been tightly bound to the trunk of the tree. She had also been given a heavy dose of laudanum. Clearly, the killer drugged her, tied her to the tree, shot the arrow, probably at close range, and then removed the bonds. This was no accident, Mr. Ward, it was cold-blooded murder!'

'But, Inspector, why would anyone wish to kill Annette?'

'That is a mystery which I intend to solve, Mr. Ward. Unhappily, the doctor disclosed another circumstance which may have a bearing on the very question you ask. His report also contains the information that the victim was with child, probably between the second and third month. We know that the steward Travis was interested in the young lady, and I shall question him again in the light of this circumstance.

'Now, Mr. Ward, I should like for you to find out, if you can, either from Miss Emily or from one of the servants, if Miss Annette had any gentlemen friends or callers during the past several months. We shall not, of course, divulge the reason for our questions.'

Accordingly, Stephen walked through the grounds of Hazelwood and approached the house on the side of the service entrance, where he found a young kitchen maid named Hannah, who had been friendly to him during his residence in the house.

Surprised to see him, the girl exclaimed, 'Have you come back, then, sir?'

'No, Hannah, I'm stopping in the village for a time. I should like to ask you a question, and I hope you will answer me truthfully.'

'Of course, sir.'

In response to Stephen's question, Hannah looked frightened, then seemed to make up her mind. 'Oh, sir, now that you ask, Miss Annette did meet with a young gentleman out beyond the gardens. When she saw me, she asked me not to tell, and gave me a brooch as a token. Ever so pretty, it is. I'm sure it's all right to tell now, isn't it, sir, now the poor lady is dead?'

'Yes, indeed. Can you tell me when this occurred?'

'Yes, sir. It were in the summer, before Miss Emily come home from her school.'

'I see. And can you describe the gentleman?'

'Oh, yes, sir. He carried a stick and was that smart-looking. His hair was black and curly, and he walked a bit odd-like.'

'Can you show me?'

The girl demonstrated a slight limp.

'I see. And did Miss Annette seem fond of the gentleman?'

'Oh, as to that, I couldn't say, sir, although they was talking very cosy, not like strangers at all.'

'Do you know if the gentleman came more than once?'

'I believe so, sir, as Miss Annette asked me several times if I thought anyone else had seen them. The servants do gossip, you know, sir, but I heard not a

word, and I didn't tell, as I was fond of Miss Annette and didn't want to cause trouble for her.'

'You're a good girl, Hannah. Thank you.' And Stephen gave the girl a coin.

When the man Travis was questioned again by Inspector Vickers, he seemed as devastated by the girl's death as his son Johnny had been. Asked if Annette had accepted his offer of marriage, he shook his head. "She said she liked and respected me but felt it would be unfair to me to marry if she did not love me." He bent his head and added softly, "I did hope that one day she might come round."

I was making a few notes when Bea's phone rang.

It was Stella Bascomb. "Claire! Please come. I need you desperately!"

"Of course, Stella. I'll come straight away."

16

FROM HER HYSTERICAL TONE ON THE TELEPHONE, I EX-
pected to find Stella in a state of disarray. Instead, she
was looking very "county," in a light wool suit with a
layer of scarves, sensible shoes, and a shopping bag at
the ready, her abundant black hair neatly pinned in a
twist, her lips and cheeks touched with healthy-
looking color.

"Claire! Thank God you're here. I've received the
call!"

"You mean—?"

"Yes. The same quacking voice, but I'm still sure
it's a woman. She wants me to put the five hundred
pounds in a letterbox within the next hour. Here are
the directions."

Her hand shaking, she held out a sheet of paper.

I read, "'Box under 5 x 5 flat rock at side of large
pool, thirty yards from south rim of Gray's Quarry,
right side of lone tree.'"

Stella's eyes pierced into mine. "You remember
Gray's Quarry, Claire?"

"Yes, of course."

"Good! Then, here's the money." She took a plastic-wrapped packet from her shopping bag. "I've rung up two friends to meet me for tea at the Kettle, so I'll have witnesses to my whereabouts. I don't want you to go down from here. It's best if you drive back into town and along the road toward the quarry. Leave your car as far away as possible, then find the box and pop this in."

I stared. "You want *me* to put the money in the box?"

"Of course, darling. I daren't do it myself, you see, in case I should be seen. There must be nothing to connect me with the whole business."

"Stella, you're mad. If someone sees me, and the connection with you is made, it would be all the same, wouldn't it?"

"No, absolutely not. The blackmailer doesn't really want to expose the transaction, as she would be criminally liable herself. It's only a precaution in case some other person should come along. If *you're* seen, there's no problem."

"Where did you get the money? If this all unravels, they can easily check for withdrawals from your bank account."

"No, no, I've provided for that. I ran up to London on Friday and pawned some old jewels I've always hated anyway. I wore old clothes, pulled a cap over my head, did a Cockney accent—it would have been great fun if it hadn't all been so ghastly. Of course I gave a false name and address. I'll never redeem the things, naturally."

"But Stella, what if a genuine letterboxer should come along and find the money before our creature gets there?"

"Oh, I doubt if this is really a registered letterbox.

The directions are much too easy, for one thing. A child of ten could find this in a snowstorm."

I tried desperately to think of a reason why I shouldn't get involved in this mess. Would I be some sort of accessory to a criminal act? Certainly, the blackmailer was committing a crime, but could the victim or an accomplice be prosecuted for paying off? I didn't know.

Too late now, anyhow. Stella was already smothering me with gratitude and zipping out the door.

With a shrug, I stuck the packet of money in my coat pocket, climbed into my car, and wound my way back toward town, taking a shortcut to the main road to Kings Abbey and turning back onto the narrow track that led toward the quarry. The morning sunshine had long since disappeared, and the day had turned into a standard overcast, the sky solidly gray; even the gorse, so cheerfully green in the sun, had faded to olive drab.

I remembered the bright day the week before when I had bicycled along this road and stopped at the quarry. I wondered if the weird lady was still making herself at home in the cave.

Wait a minute, I thought. Could she be the blackmailer? She certainly seemed to have no love for Stella, and that could extend to Oliver too. If she were a local woman, she could have known Darla Brown. But would she have seen Oliver and Darla up in the woods on a freezing day in February? And would she be clever enough to design this whole plan?

Why not? Maybe she wasn't actually a homeless person. She might be someone's relative who wandered off from time to time and then turned up again. She looked slightly mad, but that didn't rule out intelligence.

As I drove, I noticed that patches of mist were drifting here and there, but I could see through them clearly enough. Like a scrim in the theater, they softly blurred the landscape without making it invisible. Soon I came to the crossroad that led to the quarry on the left and wound its way on the right up the long hill to the Bascomb place.

This would be as good a spot as any to leave the car. I climbed out and walked along the rough track toward the quarry, trying to decide which end was south and working out that it was probably the one nearest to the path I was following. Sure enough, through the floating mist, I could see a lone tree off in the distance.

I took off over the rough, rock-strewn terrain, heading toward the tree, stepping along through patches of stubby gorse or veering around shallow pools of water. Coming up over a slight rise, I saw through the mist that beyond the tree was a large pool, surrounded by bright, jewel-green grasses.

This must be the place. Yes, there was a huge flat rock, almost square, sloping down toward the pool, the lower edge projecting out over the water.

I searched the area under the rock on the near side and saw nothing but soft green grass. My Reeboks squelched in the spongy ground as I moved around the boulder, reaching into a hollow here and there to grope for a hidden container.

Moving on to the far side, I saw, near the pool, a cluster of smaller rocks forming a barrier of sharp points and razor-like edges. The mist had laced everything with moisture, and when I tried to get a foothold on a smaller rock, my foot slipped and I came down with a painful crack on my knee.

Muttering damnation to Stella and her schemes, I

got my left foot on another sloping stone and balanced with my right hand on the edge of the big rock, getting a good look downward.

There it was—a flat metal box, far out of my reach, and tucked in so that it was only partly visible. Rather than risk slipping again on the unfriendly shards, I decided to try reaching down from the top. I circled back around the big boulder, climbed onto its flat surface, and stretched out on my stomach with my head over the edge.

From here it was no problem. I reached down and pulled up the box, wrenching the lid off the top.

Stella was right. This was not a proper letterbox. There was no notebook nor stamp inside, just the empty container.

I pulled out the packet of money and laid it inside, pressing the lid down firmly, then hung my head over the rock to put the box back where I had found it. I gave it a few extra pushes to prod it as far out of sight as possible, though I could hardly imagine hordes of people strolling by this isolated spot and finding it hidden away there.

Rubbing my still throbbing knee and muttering, "Okay. Stella, you owe me one," I got slowly to my feet.

And then it happened. Actually, three things happened first. I felt a wave of dizziness as I stood up, probably from hanging my head down over the edge of the rock. At the same time, a bird flew out of the mist and made a sharp, cawing sound as he saw me, no doubt as startled as I was to see him. I reeled back and threw up my arm as the bird swooped toward my head and flew on. And then, my foot slipped on the slick surface of the boulder.

I lost my balance and did a flip worthy of Cathy Rigby, straight into the water behind me.

It's a pretty nasty feeling at any time to drop, fully clothed, into a pool of cold water, but in this case, as my head came back up and broke the surface and I gulped for air, I realized that the foul-tasting water that poured down my face and soaked my hair reeked with a stench that made my stomach roll with nausea.

I suppose I ought to have noticed that the noxious odors floating around meant that this was a bog, but I had been too intent on what I was doing to pay much attention. Besides, I wasn't intending to sample the flavor of the water.

I struggled to get a footing, and as I stood upright, the water was about waist-deep. The big rock was out of reach, but no problem. Just swim a few strokes and I'd be out.

That was when I felt the sickening pull on my feet. I had sunk into what felt like thick mud, but when I tried to get a foot up, it wouldn't come. I looked around for something to get hold of and saw several enticing grassy mounds three or four feet away. Desperately, I stretched toward the nearer one and only managed to get another mouthful of fetid water. No hope there.

Now I tried pulling one foot slowly upward, then the other, only to feel both feet being sucked farther down into the mud. The more I struggled, the more I sank.

Sure, you're told not to struggle if you're caught in a bog. Let me tell you, that's easier said than done. Every instinct tells you that if you just give a mighty jerk, you're going to come free. In a couple of minutes, though, I did stop, because it was clear by that time that it wasn't going to work.

The water was chest-high now, and I could still feel the mud, like a living monster, laying claw-like hands on my legs and drawing me slowly down into its lair.

That's when I began to yell. "Help!" came out of my throat at the top of my voice, and I shouted a few more times before stopping for breath.

Now the mist did one of its favorite tricks and thickened into a solid mass of white. Whereas earlier I could see for a fair distance around me, everything was now blotted out, except for a tiny circle. I could see the rock, so enticingly close, the tufts of sod, and the near edges of the pool, but that was all.

I suppose I must have gone into a total panic at that point, because when I tried to shout again for help, my voice wouldn't function. My heart was banging away in my chest, and I could hear myself whispering, "Sally, Sally," while tears made paths down my cheeks, mixing with the foul-smelling water of the bog.

Then something remarkable happened. The water had just about covered my shoulders when I felt a change I couldn't quite define. My feet were so numb from the cold that at first I wasn't sure what was different.

Then I knew. *I was standing on solid ground!*

The relief was so intense that for a moment I thought: it's all over, I'm saved!

Of course, it didn't take long for the truth to wing its way to headquarters. I might not be sucked down to an immediate death, but how long could I last, standing in cold water up to my neck? I had no idea what the odds were, but I didn't think they'd go over well in Vegas.

Now I was inspired to try again calling for help. Trying to make a penetrating call without wasting my voice, I gave out a few "Helps," then waited for a while and tried again.

I didn't really want to ask myself who was likely to be strolling around this part of the moor in a heavy mist, because the answer wasn't likely to be encouraging, when suddenly it hit me. The blackmailer! She—or he, as the case may be—would probably be coming along some time this evening to retrieve the money. Whoever it was would have no reason not to help me. Even if she, to use the convenient pronoun, knew me as a friend of Stella, she could hardly admit to any knowledge of the money in the box. If only this blasted mist would clear off, my friendly blackmailer would surely turn up.

The cold was really getting to me, and my euphoria was fading fast, when a brisk breeze blew up and in minutes the mist evaporated. My first surprise was that it was still daylight. What had seemed like hours to me obviously hadn't been all that long.

I wasn't wearing my watch, having dashed off at Stella's call without bothering to put it on, and as it wasn't waterproof, it wouldn't have been much help anyhow. I had arrived at Stella's place about 4:20, left ten minutes later, parked my car at quarter to five or so, found the box, and fell into the bog somewhere around five o'clock. My best guess was that it must be 5:30 or thereabouts. This was early June, when the days were very long indeed. It wouldn't be dark till after ten o'clock. That gave me a fair chance of someone coming along, if only I could hold out against the cold. The day had started out with sunshine and the air itself was fairly mild, now the mist was gone.

I hung in, calling for help at intervals, my mood going up and down like a yo-yo. At one of the low points, when I was pretty weepy, I gave out a few shouts and incredibly, I heard a voice shouting back, "Ho!"

"Here!" I screamed, and heard an answering hoot: "Righto!"

But where was the voice coming from? I couldn't see anyone at all.

Then, over the rise beyond the lone tree, I saw a head of wild gray hair top the crest. My crazy lady from the quarry!

Blackmailer or not, she looked great to me. I've never been happier to see another human being.

Striding down toward me, she threw herself full-length on the flat rock and held out a long arm. I found that I could just get my left hand into hers. With a tight grip, she began to pull, and slowly, slowly I could feel my feet coming out of the sucking mud. Soon my other hand met both of hers, and I was drawn out of the water. With a final tug, I reached the edge of the rock and inched my way on my stomach to its heavenly safety.

As I lay panting, I heard the woman's voice above me. "Is that your car along the road?"

I nodded. "Yes. And thank you, thank you so much—"

"None o' that, now. Get up and come along."

I crawled to the edge of the rock and gingerly tried my feet on the ground.

The woman took my arm and pulled me along, scolding at me all the way.

"I don't know how you got into that bog, but a fine mess you've made o' yerself. What are ye doing out walking in the mist all alone, and no whistle nor nothin' to call for help? Don't you know a bog when you see one, miss? Didn't you smell it, now? And you might o' seen that bright green all round the place. People like you have no call to be out walking on the moor, is what I say. You stay in your fine house in the town, d'you hear?"

I nodded obediently. "Yes, I promise."

"That's all right, then. I remember you. You're the

one as come down the quarry one day, sticking your nose where you oughtn't to be."

"I'm sorry," I gasped.

Now we had almost reached my car, and she gave me a pat on the shoulder. "You get home now, fast as you can."

I called out another thank-you, but she had already turned and was striding back down the lane.

I took a picnic blanket out of my car, wrapped it around me, and started off toward Morbridge. As soon as the motor warmed, I turned on the heater and felt the exquisite warmth start to penetrate through my soaking clothes.

I tried to think what on earth I could tell Bea, but by some fantastic piece of luck, she was out. I had just popped my filthy clothes into her washer when she came in, rosy and smiling.

"I'll have my bath now," I called out to her as I dashed up the back stairs, and heard her reply, "Of course, darling. We'll go when you're ready. I know you'll love this restaurant!"

17

It was easy enough not to tell Bea about my dunking in the bog. After soaking in a heavenly bath and washing the goo out of my hair, I felt remarkably restored to normal, at least outwardly. If nightmares came, I'd deal with them later.

When we set off for the restaurant, the sun was still up there, making feeble peeps through the lackluster clouds. I'd offered to drive, and at Bea's direction, I took a road that led out onto the moor. Bea said, "Would you like to stop at Kitty Jay's grave? It's along this road, near Hound Tor."

Recalling the story told on the evening we dined with Oliver and Stella, I said I'd like that very much.

After a few miles, Bea pointed to the tor, where legend saw, in the outcroppings of rock along its crest, the shapes of a pack of hounds. Below was a farmhouse where a small sign indicated "Jay's Grave." There, in a gentle bower of trees, was a raised mound, covered with grass, with a simple headstone and a bouquet of fresh flowers.

Bea murmured, "Poor Kitty. Raised in the workhouse, then made a slavey on the farm. Poverty and cruelty are an evil combination."

We left some coins on the grave and drove on. I refrained from bringing up the subject Sally had broached with her grandmother, but Bea gave me a wistful smile. "I know what you're thinking, Claire, dear. It would have been better if the girl could have terminated her pregnancy."

"Well, she certainly wouldn't have taken her own life."

"Yes. But surely we are more tolerant today? Two centuries ago, they would have said simply that she sinned and she paid the penalty. Now, she might have gone to a shelter, then given up the child for adoption. Even in the church, she could be absolved."

I squelched the torrent of arguments that raced inside my head, trying to find a point of common ground. "You're right that society has gradually become more sympathetic to the so-called 'fallen woman.' The very fact that for more than a century Jay's grave has been kept as a symbol of compassion is better than nothing."

Bea sighed. "I remember in school reading a poem about the poor girls in Victorian London who had fallen into prostitution and drowned themselves in the Thames."

"Sounds like Thomas Hood's 'Bridge of Sighs.'" I quoted the opening lines:

> "*One more unfortunate,*
> *Weary of breath,*
> *Rashly importunate,*
> *Gone to her death!*

Take her up tenderly,
Lift her with care;
Fashioned so slenderly,
Young, and so fair!' ''

"Yes, that's the one. Actually, we were all rather deliciously shocked at the subject matter, and I remember our English mistress reproving us severely and saying it was not a matter to be treated with levity."

"Good for her."

As the terrain changed from open moorland to wooded glade, we came to an ancient inn, where we walked through a lively pub on one side of the building and on to the elegant restaurant that had recently opened. Avoiding controversial topics, we had a great dinner and drove back to Morbridge in the dusk of evening.

I expected to feel exhausted after my grim experience on the moor but found instead that I was completely wired. Bea was yawning, but when I suggested she go on to bed, she explained that she would wait till she had made her nightly visit to Mabel.

"She hasn't asked, of course, but I know she's grateful when I come in at ten o'clock and settle her in for the night."

"It's quarter past nine. Why don't you go now?"

"She likes to be in her nightdress and tucked up in bed when I arrive. If I come earlier, she might be changing and would be distressed."

It seemed to me that for a lady who hadn't asked, Mabel had made her wishes pretty clear, but Bea wouldn't see it that way, I knew.

"Look," I said, "if you're tired, I'll go. I'm going to toy with Talbot for a while anyhow."

"Oh, Claire, that would be lovely. Mabel would be pleased to see you, I know. And I'm afraid all that wine is making me dreadfully sleepy."

I shooed her off to bed with a hug, rang up Neil to say an affectionate good-night, and took up the notes I had been working on when Stella dragged me away.

Inspector Vickers's disclosures to Stephen Ward that Annette's death was not an accident but intentional murder, and that the girl was pregnant at the time of her death, occurred at the end of Volume II of Talbot's novel, thus providing the classic cliff-hanger for readers who would then eagerly pay their fee to get the third and final volume of the novel from the lending library. In a mystery novel today, the whole thing would be wound up in a few closing chapters, but the Victorians went in for stringing out the suspense and filling those fat volumes with plenty of detail.

In *The Specimen,* the inspector, who had easily diagnosed Stephen Ward's devotion to Emily Spalding, decided to make use of the young man as a private investigator, sending him off to see if he could track down Annette's mysterious gentleman caller. Before leaving, Stephen meets with Emily at the boathouse by the lake:

At three o'clock that afternoon, Emily went to meet Stephen, the warmth of the full-blown summer day adding to the flush that rose to her countenance as he approached.

'My dear, my dearest Emily.' Stephen took her hands in both of his and looked into her lovely face. 'You know of my devotion to you. I cannot conceal it; I can only say once again that I would do anything in my power to serve you.'

'Oh, Stephen, you are so good!' Emily's lips trembled, and she forced back the tears that rose to her eyes. Gesturing to her black garments, she murmured, 'Since I am in mourning, Papa will of course allow me to defer my marriage to Sir Wilfred. I can only hope that in time, he will relent.'

Stephen led her to the bench beside the boathouse, where they sat looking out over the sparkling waters of the lake. Still holding her hands in his, he spoke softly. 'If you do not care for this man, as your beloved cousin told me before her death, surely your father will not force you to fulfill an engagement to which you did not consent?'

'But he insists that I did consent! And Papa is so very frightening when he is angry.'

'Yes, I see.'

Now the tears she could no longer conceal poured from her eyes, and she withdrew her hands from Stephen's to find her handkerchief and press it against her burning cheeks.

'Annette was my dearest friend and my only champion. With her help, I might have defied Papa. Whatever shall I do without her? How could it have happend? If it was Johnny Travis, and he saw that his arrow had accidentally struck her, would he have run off without getting help? He was so fond of Annette, yet he might have been too frightened to admit to what he had done.'

Stephen said, 'Inspector Vickers is determined to solve the riddle of Annette's death. There is a line of enquiry which he has asked me to pursue for him, and I have consented to do so. It will mean that I shall be away for a time, but I shall return at the earliest possible moment. If knowing that I am devoted to your service can offer a small measure of consolation in your loss, it is all I can hope for.'

'Oh, Stephen, how kind you are!'

'God bless you, my dearest.'

Bending over her, he pressed his lips to her forehead, then turned and walked swifly away.

That afternoon, Inspector Vickers went again to the Hall to call upon Sir Wilfred Probis. Asked by the servant to wait in Sir Wilfred's 'workroom,' the inspector gazed with interest at the shelves of birds, butterflies, and other creatures of nature displayed in their glass cases. Pacing back and forth for a time, he paused for a moment by a tall window, open to the terrace, where a slight breeze offered relief from the heat of the day.

For some time, his mind busy with the questions he would put to Sir Wilfred, the inspector had heard the murmur of voices in an adjoining room without wondering about their source. Now, sounds of anger reached his ears, as the voices rose in volume. Without a moment's hesitation, he stepped through the open window onto the terrace and moved along the wall toward the room from which the voices came.

That one voice was that of Sir Wilfred he knew at once. The other was unknown to him.

'Look here, my man,' Sir Wilfred shouted, 'when you go back to the city, I want to hear that you have settled this matter for me, do you understand?'

The other voice rose to match that of Sir Wilfred. 'I can't get you more money, and that's flat.'

'We are speaking of a delay of a few months only on the other matter. Surely your principal will understand the nature of my dilemma.'

'That's as may be, Sir Wilfred. I'll do my best, but I can't hold out any hope, and that's my last word.'

The voices retreated, as Sir Wilfred evidently followed the man out of the room, still protesting. The inspector stepped neatly back through the window and was sitting quietly in a chair when the servant came in to say that Sir Wilfred would be with him in a moment.

Sir Wilfred, when he came into the workroom, showed no sign of his recent perturbation. His black hair combed neatly against his head, his face serene, the baronet smiled blandly. 'Good afternoon, inspector.'

'An interesting collection you have here, sir.'

Sir Wilfred's eyes lit with enthusiasm. 'Yes, indeed. Allow me to show you one or two items of interest which I have recently added.' And he took the inspector on a brief tour of the room, explaining his system of classification and finally pointing out a glass case containing a particularly lovely butterfly, pinned to a bed of white cotton.

'This is rather a special acquisition. But you must forgive me, inspector. Let us step out onto the terrace, where the heat is less oppressive, and you can tell me how I may be of help to you in your investigation.'

'Thank you.'

When they had settled themselves and a servant had brought a tray with glasses of a cooling drink, the inspector began. 'I have decided to speak to you on a matter which requires the utmost discretion, Sir Wilfred. I believe that I can rely upon you not to divulge to anyone what I have to say.'

'The matter will be kept in strictest confidence, I can assure you, inspector.'

'Very well. First, we have evidence which indicates that the death of Miss Annette Spalding was not accidental but was the result of premeditated murder. Further, I regret to say that the doctor's examination of the body has revealed that the lady was with child. It is possible that these two facts are related, and it is therefore of the first importance that we make every

effort to determine who is the father of the unborn child.'

Sir Wilfred nodded. *'That is a tragic circumstance indeed, inspector. Have you any clue to the identity of the man?'*

'We have learned that the young lady was seen in the grounds of Hazelwood some two or three months past, walking with a gentleman whose description we have but whose identity we do not know. Since your property adjoins that of Mr. Spalding, I thought it possible that you yourself, or perhaps one of your servants, might have seen the gentleman in question. If so, any information we can garner would be of great assistance.'

'I see. I can answer at once that I have not myself seen any stranger during that period. I shall certainly ask my butler to make discreet enquiries among the servants, without of course divulging the reason for the request.'

The inspector rose. *'Thank you very much indeed, Sir Wilfred. You may reach me at the inn in the village if you learn anything of value.'*

And the inspector took his leave.

Putting down the novel, I glanced at Bea's clock on the mantel. Almost ten o'clock. Time to go down and give Her Majesty her tea and biscuits. I picked up my coat and headed down the hill to Mabel's gabled mansion.

18

WITH THE KEY BEA HAD GIVEN ME, I OPENED MABEL Thorne's front door and stood for a moment in the entry hall, its dark wood panelling gloomy in the dim light from the stairwell. I looked for a light switch but gave up and went on up the stairs to Mabel's bedroom.

"How good of you to come, Mrs. Camden. Bea rang me to expect you."

Poor Mabel, propped by enormous pillows, looked so ill, as she held out a bony hand to greet me, that I squelched my disparaging thoughts about her character.

Following Bea's instructions, I asked Mabel if she had taken her pills, and she said she had. One for pain, one for sleep, Bea had told me, and the glazed look in Mabel's eyes suggested that the doctor had wisely given her something pretty strong.

I asked if she would like her tea now, and she nodded with a rather pathetic smile so uncharacteristic of the iron lady that I felt another stab of guilt.

I went downstairs to the kitchen, where the electric

kettle came to a boil with gratifying speed. I laid the tray with milk and sugar, and a few lemon wafers that Bea had said Mabel might like, and took the tray back up the stairs.

As I walked along the corridor toward Mabel's room, I distinctly heard a noise from the floor above me. I stopped and waited. It had sounded like footsteps, but these old houses could do plenty of creaking without any help from humans.

There it was again, a few steps, then a pause.

This wasn't a ghost or a creak. Somebody was up there, but who on earth would be roaming around Mabel's house at this hour? Thieves? Surely they would wait till the dead of night? Ten o'clock seemed a bit early for your friendly burglar.

Quickly, I settled Mabel with her tea, and, telling her I would be back in a moment, I retraced my steps along the corridor and listened.

Now I could hear the footsteps coming slowly down the stairs. It was a double flight, so the person would have to come to the landing and then turn to reach this floor.

I wasn't keen on boldly confronting the intruder, whoever it was. Instead, I slipped behind a monstrous cabinet opposite the foot of the stairs, where I could get a good look without being seen.

In the dim light cast on the stairs by a series of small shaded lamps, I saw first a pair of jean-clad legs as the figure came slowly into view. Then a stocky figure in a sweatshirt emerged, and finally the head, with long black hair and a pale face.

Harriet!

But why on earth was the girl creeping around her grandmother's house?

As she reached the floor level, I stepped forward and spoke her name.

Terrified, she whirled, and for a moment, we stood like two statues, peering into each other's faces in the semi-dark.

Then she spoke. "You're Mrs. Camden, aren't you? Mrs. Claire Camden, that is."

"Yes, I am. Have you come to see your grandmother, Harriet? She will be very glad to see you."

The girl's lips twitched nervously. "Yes. I've come to see her."

"Good," I said. "I've just taken in her tea. Why don't you go to her now, and then come down to the kitchen? I'll make another pot for us. Will you do that?"

I had used the professor/mother tone that Sally teased me about but that usually got good results, even with Sally herself at times. Harriet responded on cue with a well-brought-up "Yes, thank you," and went along to her grandmother's door.

Ten minutes later, I had made another pot and was sipping my tea when Harriet came into the kitchen, carrying Mabel's tray.

Looking at me with the hesitation of an animal that isn't sure it can trust a stranger, Harriet said, "Granny's asleep."

"I'm very glad you came, Harriet." I poured a cup and pushed it toward her, and mechanically she sat down, reached for the pitcher, and poured milk into her tea.

The girl's face twisted. "She's very ill, isn't she?"

I wasn't surprised that her first sight of Mabel since Easter had shaken her up. "Yes, I'm afraid so."

"Granny gripped my hand and told me she was very fond of me. She's never said that to me before."

Not ever, I thought, not in all those years? Was there any comfort anyone could offer?

I put my hand on her arm. "Sometimes, Harriet, people feel things they can't express. I believe your grandmother must always have loved you."

Harriet thought that one over, obviously weighing my statement dispassionately. "I don't know that she did, actually. She felt it was her duty to look after me."

Okay, Claire, I remonstrated with myself. Cut out the phony psychology.

Now Harriet said something that surprised me. "I do hope Granny will be all right for money."

Startled, I heard myself say, "But surely—" before I stopped cold.

Harriet, not noticing, went on. "She's never said, but I don't know that she has much, except for the house, of course. She could sell, couldn't she, if she should be in need?"

I nodded. "Yes, I'm sure you needn't worry on that score, my dear."

Now the girl looked at me with an oddly passive stare. "I saw you in London, didn't I?"

"Yes, at the Hayward Gallery, but you left before I could talk with you."

"Yes, I was in a hurry." The girl shivered and gulped down the hot tea, staring absently at the tabletop.

I poured her another cup and decided to try the old ploy of saying the wrong thing in the hope of being corrected. "Your grandmother tells me you worked in a shop in London—a stationer's, was it?"

"No, a chemist's."

"The one near the Queensway tube stop?"

Her mind still miles away, Harriet said, "Yes."

"But you don't live near there now?"

"No."

"Do you still see your friend Derek?"

That woke her up. Her lackluster eyes went into high voltage. "How did you know his name?"

"Your grandmother asked me to inquire after you at Trefford Place. The lady across the passage heard you call a young man by that name."

Apparently this offered some reassurance. As she slowly processed the information I could see why Darla Brown had helped Harriet with her studies when they were at school. The girl was not too swift on the uptake.

Casually, I said, "You and Darla Brown were friends. Did you see her often in London?"

Her response was curious. She looked straight into my eyes and said stiffly, "When I first went up, I saw her a few times, but not after that. We were not close friends."

I'd heard that line from her grandmother. Either her statement was true or Harriet was not about to say any more about Darla. Oh, well, I could tell Neil I tried.

Now I asked, "Will you be able to stay on for a bit now and look after your grandmother?"

At that, Harriet emerged again from her trance. Her hand holding the cup began to shake and she put it down quickly. Her eyes dilated, and she looked up toward the ceiling as if she had momentarily forgotten something which now filled her with terror.

"No, no," she whispered. "I must go now. Thank you for the tea. Good-bye."

I followed her out of the kitchen and saw her take her coat from the rack in the hall and hurry out the front door.

19

WHEN I FINALLY GOT TO BED, I DROPPED OFF LIKE A ROCK, but sometime during the night I dreamed Sally was a tiny child, lying in her crib. She was screaming and putting out her arms to me, but I couldn't reach her because something was drawing my legs down, down through the floorboards, while the lady with the wild gray hair appeared on her bicycle and waved cheerily to me as she rode by.

I slept late and woke up feeling awful. Okay. I thought, that was nightmare number one. I wondered how long I'd be plagued with these phantoms of the bog.

While I dawdled over my last cup of breakfast coffee, Bea answered her phone and came back to me. "It's Mabel. She'd like to speak to you, Claire."

Mabel's voice was quavery. "Mrs. Camden, I am most distressed. Can you tell me whether or not you spoke with my granddaughter Harriet after she left my room last evening?"

Puzzled, I said, "Yes. We had a cup of tea in the kitchen."

"And did you see her leave the house?"

"Yes, I did. She took her coat from the rack in the hall and went out the front door."

"Was she carrying anything?"

"I don't know. She may have had a handbag, but I couldn't actually see whether she did or not. She didn't have anything with her in the kitchen."

"I see."

"Is something wrong, Mrs. Thorne?"

"I'm not sure. May I speak with Bea again, please?"

To Bea, Mabel finally came out with it. A large sum of money was missing from her bedroom, and she wondered if Bea and I would help her look for it. I hurried into jeans and a sweatshirt, and we found Mabel on the sofa in the sitting room, covered with a blanket, her face gray and haggard.

"I cannot believe that Harriet would do such a thing!"

Bea made reassuring noises. "Was the money in a box, Mabel?"

"No, in a manila envelope, in the large pigeonhole of my desk in the bedroom."

"Had you always kept it in the same place?"

"Yes. It's been there for a year and more. I liked to have it by me in case of sudden need."

"When did you see it last?"

"It was there last evening before I retired for the night."

"Is it a large packet, Mabel?"

"No. It had only ten notes of one hundred pounds each."

A thousand pounds—about two thousand dollars, I thought. That could fit easily into a flat envelope.

I asked, "Is there any writing on the envelope?"

"Yes. I wrote 'In case of need' in the upper corner."

Very handy for the passing thief, I mused, and saw Bea's face reflect the same thought.

Now Bea said, "What about your household helper, Mabel? Might she have taken it?"

"Not if I saw it last evening."

In the end, Bea and I searched through the orderly desk and in other places in Mabel's bedroom. When we found nothing, Mabel agreed that Bea should inform the local police.

I went back to Bea's place and rang Neil at the police station in Kings Abbey. "You'll be hearing about the robbery," I told him, "but I want to let you know also what I learned from Harriet last evening."

I told him everything I could remember about the night before, from the time I entered Mabel's house till I saw Harriet go out the door.

When I finished, Neil asked me to hold, and I could hear him giving instructions for someone to go up to London at once and check out all the chemist's shops near the Queensway tube station for information about Harriet Thorne.

"You may have given us the best lead yet, my love. Clever of you to ferret that out of our Harriet."

I smiled modestly. "No extra charge."

Neil went on. "Now, as for the robbery, about how long were you and Harriet in the kitchen over your tea?"

"Not more than ten or fifteen minutes at most."

"Mmm. I presume Harriet could have slipped the envelope into a pocket of her jeans, or popped it into her coat before coming down to the kitchen. You say she was nervous?"

I thought that one over. "Yes, but not nervous in

that way, if you know what I mean. She would have to be a good actress to coolly rob her granny and then waltz downstairs for a little chat with me. Frankly, I doubt if she's clever enough to pull it off."

"A trifle dim, is she?"

"Yes, that's my impression."

"I see. Well, then, the other possibility is that an intruder enters the house during the precise interval when you two were in the kitchen, finds Mabel sleeping soundly, takes the money, and nips out without being seen or heard. Rather improbable, wouldn't you say?"

"The whole thing's improbable, Neil. I wonder where Harriet went after she left the house? I suppose you'll be looking for her."

"That, my dear one, is a classic understatement. We wanted to see her before. Now we shall no doubt run her picture in the news and hope to ferret her out."

"You believe she stole the money from her grandmother, then?"

"I wouldn't go that far, but we certainly need to find her."

I grinned. "I know. You want her 'to assist the police in their enquiries.' Double-talk for 'You're our chief suspect.'"

"More or less. But we'll pursue other leads as well. The local chaps will go door-to-door there in the neighborhood. People notice things in a small town, as you know. We may get something useful."

I smiled wryly. "I don't suppose *I'm* a suspect?"

"Some idiot will inevitably suggest that, of course."

Smugly, I said, "I know a Detective Superintendent who can testify to the purity of my character."

"I can testify to more than that, my sweet, but not here in my office."

I smiled, and Neil went on. "You say that Harriet wondered if her grandmother was short of money. Would she have known the lady kept this amount of cash lying about?"

"I wouldn't have thought so, and I'm certain Mabel wouldn't have told her."

Now Neil said, "We'll need a statement from you as a witness. Normally, I'd ask you to come into the station, but I can have this typed up and send someone over with it for your signature."

"Do you mean the station in Kings Abbey?"

"Yes."

"Well, look, I'll be going through on my way back to London. Why don't I just stop in and sign it there?"

Half an hour later, I followed Neil's directions to the police station in Kings Abbey. Wondering if the station was housed in an ivy-covered cottage or at least a renovated Edwardian mansion, as is sometimes the case in English towns, I found instead a two-story stucco of recent construction, totally lacking in architectural charm.

I gave my name, and Neil appeared at the desk. With straight-faced solemnity, he said, "Good afternoon, Mrs. Camden. If you'll come this way, please."

"Thank you."

He led the way to his private office, where he had obviously added some personal touches to the institutional decor. I noticed a few prints on the walls, a flowering plant in the corner by the window, an Oriental carpet, and a rather nice walnut desk, none of which looked as if they had been provided by the Constabulary.

While we waited for my statement to be prepared, Neil's phone rang constantly and officers came and went with questions and reports. At one phone message, he wrote rapidly, giving me a look which said something interesting had come in.

When he rang off, he said, "Thank God for the English pub, producing people walking about at night. Sometime after half-past ten last evening, an elderly gentleman was walking up Abbey Road, returning home after his last pint at the local, and saw a young woman with long, dark hair run from a house clearly identified as the Thorne place. She dashed across the road, but he couldn't see her after that."

Presently an officer came in and handed me a copy of my statement, asking me to read it over and sign it if I believed it to be accurate. I was impressed with the detail Neil had managed to include from the notes he had taken, and was just signing the paper when his phone rang again.

A longer conversation this time, with Neil asking questions and nodding vigorously. When he finished, he offered to walk me to my car, waiting till we were out in the parking lot before asking me if I had ever seen a rather odd-looking woman, with unkempt gray hair, riding a bicycle in Morbridge.

Longing to say it sounded like the woman who had saved my life, I managed a casual "Yes, I have. May I ask why?"

"Officially, no, but I shall tell you anyhow. A lady out walking her dog on Abbey Road at a quarter past ten or so last evening saw a woman of that description ride her bicycle up the drive of Mabel Thorne's house, but instead of going to the door, she went round the side of the house and peered through a window. Our witness thought it odd but not alarming, so she merely walked on."

"Could she see the woman clearly in the dark?"

"She was asked that question and said she had seen

the woman on several occasions in the neighborhood of Abbey Road in the daylight hours and recognized her as the same person."

"I see."

"Where did you see her, Claire?"

"The first time it was in Abbey Road, as I was leaving Bea's house one day last week."

"And you saw her again elsewhere?"

I hesitated, then decided I'd better come clean, without revealing anything about Stella and the blackmail. "Yes, I saw her one day at Gray's Quarry, where she seemed to be taking shelter in the cave. I think she may be one of those homeless persons who's mentally disturbed but quite harmless."

I was sure my bicycle lady, as I had come to think of her, couldn't have robbed Mabel, and maybe if the police picked her up, she'd be referred to an agency that could give her some help.

I got into my car and Neil leaned on the window ledge. "I'm not sure when I'll get up to London now. Things are getting a bit hectic here."

"No problem. As John Donne so aptly said, 'Dull sublunary lovers' can't bear to be parted:

'But we, by a love so much refin'd,/Care less eyes, lips, and hands to miss.'"

Neil laughed. "But don't forget, my dearest one, Donne also said: 'Love's mysteries in souls do grow,/But yet the body is his book.'"

I smiled. "He was right about that!" And I waved goodbye.

20

IT WAS A RELIEF TO BE BACK TO MY DESK IN BEDFORD
Square. I answered the messages on my machine,
making a date for the following week to see a film with
an old friend and putting off another till I knew what
Neil's plans were. Then I collapsed in front of the
television with my dinner plate, watched the news,
deplored the number of appalling sitcoms that had
invaded the sceptered isle, and went to bed early.

No nightmares of the bog, I reflected with relief
next morning. I wrote a first draft of commentary on
the passages in *The Specimen* that I had worked on in
Devon. Now I was ready for the scene in which, for
the first time, Emily Spalding dares to stand up to her
father. Talbot had to tread carefully here. Fathers were
the lords and masters of their domains, and the
lending libraries didn't want to disseminate any prop-
aganda to the contrary.

Even more difficult was the problem of dealing with
pregnancy. Because Annette was already dead, it was
easier to defend her posthumously, apparently

through the unspoken rule that she had "paid the price." The men who seduced young women didn't have any dues to pay to society, but that hasn't changed much even today.

Sir Wilfred Probis must have been putting the pressure on Emily's father to get on with the marriage, for soon after Stephen Ward's departure in search of Annette's mysterious visitor, George Spalding summoned his daughter to his study:

When Emily saw the frown of displeasure on her father's face, she trembled, wondering what she might have done to offend him.

'Now, then, Emily,' he began, 'I have something to say to you. Sir Wilfred would like to set a date three months hence for your nuptials. May I tell him I have your consent?'

'But Papa, that is not possible. I am in mourning for my cousin.'

Now her father's face took on a scowl more dreadful than any she had ever seen. 'That is no longer a consideration, Emily. Information has come to me, the nature of which I do not wish to divulge to you, but which negates any respect you may owe to the memory of your cousin.'

Aghast, Emily stared at her father. 'Whatever do you mean, Papa?'

'I have told you all you need to know, Emily. I expect you to obey my wishes without further question.'

Emily felt a tide of anger surge through her body. She stood before her father, hands clenched at her sides. 'If I am old enough to be married, Papa, I am old enough to be told what information you have about my cousin that could cause you to say what you did.'

A look of cold triumph appeared on George Spalding's countenance. 'Very well, Emily, since you

*insist, I shall tell you. At the time of her death, your
cousin Annette was expecting a child.'*

At the shock produced by this news, Emily nearly
crumpled to the floor at her father's feet, but somehow
she found the courage to stand her ground. *'I do not
know how this came about, Papa, but I know that my
cousin was all that is kind and good. I shall always
honor her memory!'*

And Emily fled from the room.

Here, the novel shifts to Stephen Ward's travels on
the trail of the dapper man with the limp who had
visited Annette at Hazelwood. When he finally
catches up with him, he proves to be a friend of
Annette's father, who had sometimes been involved
in confidence schemes with the older man but who
had been friendly to Annette throughout her lonely
childhood. Always in need of money, he had come to
Hazelwood in the hope of scrounging funds from the
girl and had gone away when he became convinced
she had none.

As for having engaged in any intimacy with
Annette, the man hooted, telling Stephen he "would
never have tried it on," as that would have cooked his
goose for getting any money from her. She had been
grateful to him in her youth, he explained, but had
never fancied him in the least.

It is at this point that Inspector Vickers makes the
discovery that unravels the mystery. Talbot gives an
admirable picture of Inspector Vickers's painstaking
skill in the pursuit of truth in the face of wealth and
title. Refusing to be intimidated by George Spalding
or taken in by Sir Wilfred Probis, Vickers is portrayed
as an astute judge of character. He believes both
Johnny Travis and his father when it would be conve-

nient to lay the blame on one or both. He believes Emily when she describes the essential goodness of her cousin Annette.

In an interview with Emily, the inspector provides the final clue when he asks if Annette kept a journal. Emily replies that she had on a few occasions seen Annette writing in a green leather volume with a silver clasp:

'Do you know where that journal was kept, Miss Spalding?'

'I believe I saw her put it into a locked compartment in her wardrobe.'

'Shall we look for it now?'

'Yes, of course.'

Emily led the way to her cousin's room and opened the mahogany wardrobe, pointing to a small compartment inside.

'Where may we find the key?'

'That I do not know.'

Inspector Vickers gave a brisk gesture around the room. 'I believe we must find that key, Miss Spalding. Do I have your permission?'

'Yes, and my help.'

Together they went through the drawers and cupboards in the room, Emily's heart beating painfully as she touched Annette's clothing and the trinkets she had loved. In a pigeonhole in the small rosewood desk, Emily found a key and held it up.

'This may be the one, Inspector.'

'Let us try.'

Emily held her breath as she inserted the key into the little cabinet and gave it a turn. It opened easily, but when she reached inside, she found nothing. The cabinet was empty.

Now Inspector Vickers stood deep in thought, his eyes moving slowly around the room. At last he spoke. 'Something happened to cause Miss Annette to take her diary from this cabinet. Will you tell me, Miss Emily, everything you can remember that occurred on the day before your cousin's death?'

'Yes, gladly.'

Emily gestured to the pair of chairs where she had sat so often with her cousin in happier days, and the inspector sat quietly until she was ready to speak.

'That morning, I looked out of the window and saw my cousin walking in the garden with Sir Wilfred Probis. They were talking earnestly for a time; then I saw him give her a sort of pat on the arm, in a kindly way. After that, I turned back into my room and did not see them again.'

'And later that day?'

'Sir Wilfred came to tea, and my father said something to Annette which humiliated her.'

'Can you tell me what it was?'

Emily's eyes burned with indignation. 'He said Travis, the steward, had come to him expressing his desire to marry Annette, and Papa asked her, in the presence of Sir Wilfred, if Travis had spoken to her about it. I protested but Papa went on, not realizing the pain he was causing in speaking of her affairs so openly.'

'And how did your cousin respond?'

'She said nothing at first. Sir Wilfred remarked that Travis was a fine fellow. Then Annette stood up and said in a low voice that, as she was a penniless beggar, she should be glad of any offer. Then she left the room. I shall never forget her words.'

The inspector leaned forward, his nose sharp as a hunting dog's, but his eyes benevolent. 'Now, Miss

Emily, I should like to ask you a question which you may not wish to answer.'

'I shall try if I can, Inspector.'

'It is this: your father tells me you are betrothed to Sir Wilfred Probis. May I ask if this is consonant with your own wishes?'

Now Emily's eyes filled with tears. 'No, sir, I do not wish to marry Sir Wilfred.'

'May I ask if your cousin was aware of this circumstance?'

'I did not tell her at once, as my father had forbidden me to speak of it until I should give my consent.'

'Did you at any time tell Miss Annette about this?'

'Yes.'

'Was this on the day before you saw your cousin and Sir Wilfred in the garden?'

'Yes.'

'And what was your cousin's opinion as to your engagement?'

Emily's voice shook. 'She was surprised. Then she became agitated and told me I must not marry him, that it was wrong!'

'Did she explain what she meant by this?'

'No, she was feeling rather ill and I did not press her. I believe she meant that it was wrong to marry if one did not love. You see, she had refused Travis's offer because she did not care for him in that way.'

Now the inspector sat in silence, staring at the floor. Then he raised his head and surveyed the room as he had done before. 'We must find that diary, Miss Emily,' he said briskly. 'Your cousin obviously went to some pains to prevent its discovery. She removed it from the small cabinet in the wardrobe and placed it—where? One might say it could be anywhere in the house or grounds of Hazelwood, yet I am certain she would have secreted the object here in her own room.'

Emily watched as the inspector climbed on a stool and examined the top of the wardrobe, evidently finding nothing. He felt behind the heavy draperies at the windows and along the top of the valance board, then raised the mattress of the bed and searched there as well as under the frame of the bed. At last, he lifted the corners of the carpets that covered large segments of the room.

Between Annette's bed and the window lay a Turkey carpet which the inspector rolled back carefully. On his hands and knees, he felt along the floor. Suddenly, Emily heard an exclamation of delight.

She stepped forward in time to see him lift a corner of a floorboard, revealing a small recess. 'Here we are, Miss Emily!' He lifted out a book bound in dark green leather and handed it to her. When he had replaced the board, the floor looked completely undisturbed.

The inspector rolled back the carpet and stood up. 'I believe this is the diary?'

Emily's heart beat rapidly. 'Yes, sir, it is, but we shall have to find the key to the clasp.'

Unhappily, despite their best efforts, they could find nothing that would fit the tiny lock.

Emily sighed in despair. 'What shall we do, sir?'

'This should present no problem.' The inspector reached into a pocket of his coat and extracted a pointed tool, which he inserted into the lock. After a quick twist, the clasp sprang open.

The inspector nodded. 'Here we are, then! This is what I propose, Miss Emily. I have no wish to intrude upon the privacy of your cousin except as it affects the present investigation. May I ask that you read what is contained here and then convey to me any information which will assist me in that endeavor, omitting whatever is not relevant?'

'Gladly, sir. I shall do so at once.'

'*Very good. I shall be at the inn. If you will send someone for me, I shall return on the instant.*'

'*Will you not wait in the house, inspector?*'

*In a level tone, without rancor, Vickers replied, '*Your father does not welcome my presence here, Miss Emily. I am better in the village.*'*

And with that he took his leave.

21

MARKING A PASSAGE IN MY COPY OF *THE SPECIMEN*, I
reflected on the fondness of Victorian ladies for
keeping daily journals. As readers, they adored long
entries from such diaries in the popular novels of the
day, often emulating in their own journals the
highflown style supplied by the novelists. In lives
where the most memorable incident of the week might
be a visit from the local clergyman, the romantic
episodes of fiction offered vicarious thrills to many a
mundane life.

Mary Louise Talbot was quite willing to provide her
readers with plenty of what they liked, as the passages
from Annette's journal testify. At the same time,
Talbot delivers the clear message that young women
were particularly vulnerable to the machinations of
men whom they trusted because they were "gentlemen." Even Annette, who had known near-poverty at
times, was still the daughter of a gentleman, con-artist
though he was, and had evidently been protected

against any sexual advances from the men in their circle.

Now I picked up the novel at the point where Inspector Vickers had left the house. Emily Spalding took Annette's green leather journal to her own room, where she sat by the window and opened the book. The first entry was dated in November of the preceding year, when her cousin had come to live at Hazelwood.

In Annette's firm hand, the first page read, "I shall begin a new volume, as this is the beginning of a new life for me." A series of entries described her pleasure in the beauties of the countryside and in the felicities of life at Hazelwood contrasted with the discomforts of her former life. "I am not wearing mourning for my father, as I do not wish to be a hypocrite. At first I feared that Uncle would protest or perhaps insist that I wear the black garb, but he seems not to have noticed. He is much preoccupied with his own thoughts and pays little attention to my presence, which is in some respects a boon."

This came as no surprise to Emily, who had grown up with her father's indifference.

With the coming of the Christmas holidays, Annette wrote glowingly of the return from school of her "dear, dear Emily," expressing her joy in finding at last someone whom she could love as a sister.

After Emily's return to school, Annette wrote, "I am so grateful to my dear cousin for allowing me to make use of her dressmaker. My wardrobe is becoming quite worthy of a resident of Hazelwood!"

Soon, entries began to appear in praise of their neighbor, Sir Wilfred Probis. "He is a fine-looking man, and most intelligent." In January, "Today I visited the Hall for the first time and Sir W. showed me his splendid collection of natural specimens. When I shuddered at the long pins that pierced the butterflies, he assured me the lovely creatures had been painlessly slain before the pins were inserted."

By February, Sir Wilfred featured in many entries. "This evening, as he saw me to the door of the dining room, he told me I was looking very handsome. I was wearing my new green velvet and am glad if it becomes me." A few days later, "Sir W. pressed my hand as we said good-night. I felt a flush on my cheeks, but Uncle was looking the other way and did not see."

A number of such compliments occurred at intervals until early March, at which time Sir Wilfred went off to the Continent for an extended tour in the company of an old friend from his school days. Emily's return for the Easter holiday absorbed all of Annette's attention for the next three weeks, and Emily's eyes filled with tears as she read of the many happy occasions they had shared during that time.

Meanwhile, Annette had recorded an incident involving Johnny Travis and her efforts to get him out of a scrape, eliciting his solemn promise not to err again. Then began regular mentions of Johnny's father, his kindness to her, his gratitude for her help with Johnny, and so on.

Twice during his absence, Sir Wilfred had sent brief notes to Annette, one describing the beauty of Alpine scenery, another expressing his scientific interest in the German classification of insects. It was obvious from her entries in the journal that she had treasured these missives. Now a third letter came for her:

20 May. *Sir Wilfred is coming home, perhaps in two weeks' time! He has written to me from Paris that he has thought of me often during his travels*

*and that he has met not a single lady whose
charms compare with mine. I shall protest that he
must not pay me such compliments. . . .*

5 June. *We have had sunshine for three days, in
time to welcome Sir W. home. This afternoon he
walked over in time for tea. I have seldom seen
Uncle so animated. He is extremely fond of Sir
Wilfred. Having no son of his own, as he is wont to
say, he has found a surrogate in our neighbor. Sir
W. was courteous to me but gave no sign of the
admiration expressed in his letter from Paris.
However, as he was taking his leave, he said to
Uncle, 'May I ask Miss Annette to accompany me
as far as the lake? The day is too glorious to be
missed.'*

*Uncle nodded genially, saying, 'By all means,
my dear sir.' As I took up my parasol, I felt my
heart beating and hoped the color was not rising in
my face. We walked in silence along the path
toward the lake, and when we reached the little
glade that passes under the lacing branches of the
elms, Sir W. remarked on his pleasure at being in
England again. 'There is much to be admired on
the Continent,' he said, 'and one can live very
cheaply there. One meets interesting people, especially at the watering-places, but there is nothing
to compare with our English rose.'*

*I looked on either side of the path and, seeing no
roses, I glanced up at him enquiringly. He stopped
and stood looking down at me. 'Not that kind,
Annette. You are the rose I mean. You are not a
pale pink, like those young ladies who have no
spirit. You are a deep red rose, full of richness and
beauty. I have carried your image with me, the
dark enchantment of your eyes and hair.' My*

parasol had fallen back, and he put his hand on my forehead, lifting a strand of hair that had escaped from its moorings.

For a moment, I stood transfixed, my heart beating wildly. Then I managed to smile and say firmly, 'I thank you, Sir Wilfred, but I must say good-bye,' and I turned and walked quickly back toward the house.

I had meant to protest against such compliments, but I could not bring myself to do so. It was so sweet to me to hear his voice, to see the ardor in his eyes, as he spoke to me. Yes, I may confess it to myself alone. I believe he loves me! He could not speak like this to me unless he is sincere. Of that I am certain.

8 June. Uncle and I were invited to dine at the Hall this evening. Sir W. was most cordial to both of us but, until the end of the evening, he gave no sign to me of the words he had spoken in the glade three days ago. When we had taken our tea in the drawing room, he proposed a brief stroll in the grounds, to which Uncle protested that he was too comfortable to stir, saying, 'You may take Annette if you like.'

At that, Sir W. smiled at me and offered his arm. We walked across the terrace and into a rose garden beyond a high hedge, where he stopped beside a bush heavy with blossoms. Darkness was falling, but there was yet enough light to see the roses nearest to where we stood. He took my hand and said, 'My dear Annette, I have looked forward to this moment.'

He stooped and broke off a rose. In the dusky light I could see the deep red hue of its petals. He said, 'This is the bloom I treasure most dearly. Except for this.' And he bent and kissed me lightly on the forehead. Before I could speak, he took my elbow and gently led me out of the garden, saying, 'I must return you to your uncle.'

He has spoken no word of love to me as yet, but his actions tell me what I know in my heart. I believe he is too honourable to make a declaration until he has spoken to Uncle and gained his permission. I know now that I love him too, but I shall keep my secret until it can be told to the world.

I do wonder how Uncle will take the news. To him I am merely a poor relation, but he cannot deny that I have the same blood as he. I am, after all, a Spalding. Poverty cannot change that. Father and Uncle were first cousins, with a common grandfather. Furthermore, I believe Uncle is fond enough of Sir W. to wish for his happiness.

13 June. *The die is cast! There is no doubt now that Sir Wilfred means to marry me!*

It all began yesterday when Sir W. invited me to ride with him. He brought a horse for me to Hazelwood and the groom helped me to mount in the side-saddle. I had warned Sir W. that I was not an experienced horsewoman, but he laughed and said no matter, he would teach me what I needed to know.

The horse seemed unduly lively to me, but we went along merrily enough, following the path through the woods, past the lake, and into the grounds of the Hall. Suddenly, something must have frightened my horse, because he leaped forward and began to dash away. Sir W., who was following, brought his own horse up beside mine and attempted to grasp my reins, but before he could do so, my horse galloped off again.

I was terrified and held to the saddle as tightly as

I could, but in the end I could not keep my balance and was thrown off. I fell into a bed of fern, which must have helped to cushion my body, but as I landed, my head struck against the trunk of a tree and I twisted my ankle most painfully.

Sir W. knelt by my side and took me in his arms, and I am certain I saw tears in his eyes as he asked if I were hurt. At first, I said it was nothing, but when I stood and tried to walk, I swayed dizzily and found I could not place weight on my left foot. As we were not far from the Hall, Sir W. lifted me onto his horse and led me back toward the house, where he carried me inside and placed me on a sofa in a small sitting room, sending a servant to the village for the doctor.

By the time the doctor arrived, my ankle was already swelling. He bound it lightly and left instructions for placing it in cool water, but when I suggested that I could now go home, Sir Wilfred protested. 'I am concerned about the injury to Miss Spalding's head, doctor. Would it not be better for her to remain here until you can examine her again tomorrow?'

The doctor agreed that it would indeed be advisable for me to remain as quiet as possible, and so it was arranged. A servant was sent to Hazelwood to inform Uncle and to bring the things I would require for the night.

Sir W. gave instructions that the "Gainsborough room" be prepared for me, and again he took me in his arms, carrying me up the stairs and down a long corridor. As I put my arms round his neck to help support my weight, and laid my head against his shoulder, I felt a sense of safety I had rarely known in my life before. This man would protect me and care for me; his love would cushion me from life's vicissitudes.

As he placed me on the bed, I looked round at the room, with its blue hangings. On the wall opposite hung a small print of a snow scene, the faded wall covering making a border around its edges. I saw no other pictures on the walls and asked with a smile, 'Where is the Gainsborough?'

Sir W. glanced about carelessly. 'Someone must have taken it away,' he said with a shrug.

He left me then to rest, saying he would return after dinner to enquire after my progress.

Hannah, the kitchen maid from Hazelwood, was sent with my things and helped me into my nightdress. As I had no maid of my own, I had made rather a friend of Hannah, so that if I did need help, I could now and then ask for her if Cook gave her leave.

She helped me to place my foot in a deep basin of water for a time, then brushed my hair and settled me in the big canopy bed, saying, 'Oh, Miss Annette, you do look that lovely!'

I thanked her and sent her back promptly, lest Cook be angry, but her remark pleased me and I promised her a favor when I should return to Hazelwood.

I must have slept then, for I was awakened by the arrival of my dinner tray. When I tried to sit upright, I was aware of the dizziness I had felt earlier, and now the pain in my ankle became very troublesome. The doctor had given me a liquid to take if the pain should return, and I poured out the amount he had prescribed and took it with the glass of wine on my tray.

When the servant came to take my tray, I must have slept again, as I have no recollection of anything until I opened my eyes and saw Sir W. sitting beside my bed. Darkness must have fallen, as no light was visible through the closed shutters of the windows.

He took my hand and looked into my eyes with deep concern. I assured him I felt no pain, and he said that made him very happy indeed. He poured a glass of wine for each of us and lifted me up against the pillows so that I might drink. I felt myself floating in a magical dreamland, and when the wine was gone and he took me in his arms, his kisses seemed to be a natural expression of his love.

For yes, now at last he told me that he loved me!

What happened then I cannot describe, I can only say that he made me his own, to love and to cherish for ever and ever.

I came back to Hazelwood in the carriage this morning, my heart overflowing with gladness. I expect he will come to speak with Uncle today, to ask for my hand. Then at last I shall be able to tell my dear Emily of my happiness.

22

WHEN I BROKE FOR LUNCH ON WEDNESDAY, THE DAY AFTER
my return from Devon, I left Emily Spalding holding
her cousin Annette's diary and went downstairs to the
foyer of the building to pick up my mail. Back
upstairs, I went through that day's collection and
found a letter from a Talbot descendant who had
kindly answered my inquiry about her famous ances-
tor. She regretted that she had no letters to or from
Mary Louise but mentioned an uncle whose family
might have documents that would be useful to me.
The uncle, who had died some years ago, had lived at
an address north of Regent's Park.

This was exactly the kind of lead I loved to get.
Sleuthing around among birth and death records,
parish registers, and the like was sheer pleasure,
especially with the chance of tracking down fresh
material. Hoping that the uncle's death certificate
might give me a lead to other family members, I
checked my map of the boroughs of London and

confirmed that the uncle's address at the time of his death was in the Borough of Camden, the same as my own. I liked the coincidence of the name, although I knew there was no connection with Miles's family.

After a quick cheese sandwich and an apple, I set off for a brisk walk up to the Euston Road, where the Town Hall occupies two vast buildings. In the newer building, in the office where births, marriages, and deaths are recorded, I gave the name and the approximate death date of my subject, and took a seat.

Looking absently around the familiar, L-shaped waiting room, I glanced at the large glass case on the wall where notices of forthcoming marriages were posted. Remembering that Neil said the police had checked each London borough for Darla Brown's name and found nothing, I walked over to the case to have a look. Could they have missed something? Not likely. I understood these were posted only for a month before being taken down. Too late for Darla and her fiancé.

Running my eye down the columns, I saw that the "posting" consisted of the top of each application, folded so that only the basic information of name, age, address, and so on was revealed. I saw nothing about Darla Brown, but an entry in the second column stopped me cold.

"HARRIET L. THORNE," I read, "Age: 18. *Marital status:* Spinster. *Occupation:* Shop assistant."

I smiled at the archaic term "spinster," still used in official forms.

Below Harriet's name, I read:

"DEREK J. MALONE. Age: 24. *Marital status:* Bachelor. *Occupation:* Unemployed."

Well, well. So Harriet and her Derek were planning to be married.

Then it hit me. Derek *Malone?*

Surely not Darla's prison officer friend Malone? We'd never heard his first name.

I remembered from the inquest that Darla had worn a locket with two hearts, each with the letter "D" inscribed. The story that these meant "double love" wasn't very convincing. Much more likely it was some lover's name.

With a shrug, I looked back at the certificate form for Harriet and Derek. After "Place of residence," both applicants were listed as living at 28 Orcutt Street, No. 3, NW 1. "Period of residence" for Derek was one month; for Harriet one week. At last, an address for Harriet. I jotted it down and went back to my seat.

If this *were* the same "Derek," Harriet could certainly have met him when she got together with Darla in London. Her story was that she saw Darla only when she first came up to the city. In that case, would she have been in touch with Darla's friend Derek months later at the time Darla's body was found in a bog on Dartmoor?

But what if she had in fact continued to see Darla from time to time? She would no doubt have kept this from her grandmother, just as she had concealed the extent of her friendship with Darla while she was still living at home in Morbridge.

Another question. Would Derek Malone have transferred his affection from Darla to Harriet so soon after Darla's death? Why not? Some might say that after shapely Darla, Harriet's attractions wouldn't be overwhelming, but there's no accounting for tastes.

I was called to the window and handed the book containing the death certificate I had come to see. Hastily, I made notes of the information I needed, handed in the book, and went out to the Euston Road, where the usual traffic roared and surged. A taxi cruised toward me and I hopped in, giving the driver the address in Orcutt Street where Harriet and Derek were listed as living.

Since the house was somewhere in the borough, I knew it couldn't be unreasonably far. From the postal code, NW1, it was probably north of the Euston Road. My driver had to move along for several streets before crossing over the divided thoroughfare. Then he turned back and maneuvered through the crawling mass until we reached the road that lies between the old brick mountain of St. Pancras Station and the modern glass and concrete structure of King's Cross.

For five minutes or so we twisted through neighborhoods that looked like candidates for a documentary on poverty. While I hadn't expected to find Harriet and Derek living in luxury, this area was pretty depressing. Harriet's bedsit in Queensway, where I had talked to her neighbor across the passage, may have been on the seedy side, but it was a palace compared to 28 Orcutt Street.

I asked the driver to wait and picked my way through the litter on the pavement to a battered front door that hung askew. Graffiti decorated the interior walls, and as I moved farther inside, foul odors drifted around in the airless corridor.

I found number 3 on the ground floor at the back and knocked firmly. Nothing. This was no time for subtlety. I pounded hard.

Shuffling feet, fumbles at a door chain, and a man, red-eyed and unshaven, peered out at me, exuding alcoholic fumes.

"Is Derek Malone here?" I asked.

"It's Malone you want, is it?"

"Yes, please. Does he live here?"

The eyes looked at me craftily. "He might do. Why don't you step in, little lady?"

Look, Claire, I said to myself, don't be stupid. Let the police handle this one.

Politely I said, "No, thank you, I'll try later," and marched back outside to my taxi.

Back in the flat, I thought of phoning Neil to give him the Orcutt Street address but decided to wait. He was due to call me that evening. I could tell him then. Since Harriet and Derek didn't in fact live there, the police would have to pry information from the drunken lout who had opened the door to me. Good luck to them, I thought.

I curled up in my favorite chair and went on with my rereading of *The Specimen*.

23

READING AGAIN THE SCENE IN THE NOVEL WHERE ANNETTE is seduced by Sir Wilfred Probis, I reflected on how adroitly Mary Louise Talbot had circumvented the act of sexual intercourse. On strictly moral grounds, there was no doubt Annette should have known better, just as little Kitty Jay, whose grave we had visited, had known she might be in big trouble if she succumbed to her lover, whoever he was.

What Talbot did was fairly daring. She didn't cop out altogether by having Annette drugged and unconscious when the act took place. The doctor's prescription—probably laudanum—in combination with the wine, certainly lowered the girl's resistance, but she knew quite well what had happened to her. She did not protest that she was raped. On the contrary, she regarded it as an act of love.

Thirty years later, Thomas Hardy went a step further in *Tess of the D'Urbervilles,* where Tess is seduced by Alec although she does *not* in fact love him. Alec finds her sleeping on a bed of leaves in the forest at night, and Hardy asks with poetic delicacy, "Why was it that upon this beautiful feminine tissue, sensitive as gossamer and practically blank as snow as yet, there should have been traced such a coarse pattern as it was doomed to receive?"

For a century, critics have quibbled over what happened to Tess, some referring to rape, others to seduction. Many have missed the fact that Tess herself makes no claim of rape. On the contrary, she stays on with Alec for a month or more after the fatal night in the Chase, evidently submitting to him reluctantly from time to time. It is when she realizes she cannot love him that she leaves him to go home to her family. Hardy makes this explicit when Tess tells Alec, "'If I had ever sincerely loved you, I should not so loathe and hate myself for my weakness as I do now! My eyes were dazed by you for a little, and that was all.'"

No wonder Hardy's subtitle, "A Pure Woman," enraged the Mrs. Grundys but gave an enormous boost to the growing enlightenment concerning the status of women.

I was jotting some notes when the front door buzzer sounded and I pressed the intercom on the wall.

"Mrs. Camden?"

"Yes."

"It's Harriet Thorne. May I come and talk to you?"

"Of course, Harriet. Come up one flight." And I buzzed the door release.

It took a while before I could get Harriet to tell me what she had come for. She was looking nervous and frightened, but that was no surprise, as her picture had already appeared in the newspapers the evening before. I offered tea and when she accepted, I invited her into the kitchen, remembering we had sat together in Mabel Thorne's kitchen the night her grandmother was robbed.

While I filled the pot, I asked gently, "Do you know the police would like to interview you, Harriet?"

"Yes, I know."

I put out a plate of wafers and saw, as she reached for one, that she wore a gold band on her left hand. Were she and her Derek already married? I'd find out soon enough, no doubt. I wondered how on earth she knew where I lived, but that could wait too.

"You needn't be afraid to let the police know where you are, Harriet. If you have done nothing wrong, they will just talk to you and let you go."

She looked at me with mournful eyes. "You don't understand."

I poured out our tea. "What is it I don't understand?"

Now her eyes swam with tears. "I'm so afraid, Mrs. Camden. I don't know what to do."

I gave her some time, stirring my tea and waiting for her to go on. At last she said, "Do they think I took my grandmother's money? I *didn't*, Mrs. Camden. I didn't even know she had any money in the house."

"I'm inclined to believe you, Harriet, but you must see the police need to talk to you about it."

"They might not believe me."

Now I tried sweet reason. "Look, Harriet, you can't hide from the police forever, you know, and it will look much better if you come forward on your own than if you wait till you're apprehended. Staying away makes you look guilty, even if you're not."

Now I got that "You don't understand" look again and I said, "There's something else, isn't there?"

She looked so miserable I put my hand over hers as I would have done with Sally, and this motherly gesture seemed to break the spell.

Harriet took a deep breath and let it out on a

half-sob. "Oh, Mrs. Camden, I must talk to someone. I feel I'm going mad, and you were so kind to me that night at Granny's. I've promised Derek not to tell anyone anything, but I can't bear it any longer."

I waited, but I could see how hard it was for the girl to get started on her story, whatever it was. Carefully, I asked, "Harriet, is your friend Derek the same young man who was Darla's—er—friend also?"

This didn't seem to alarm her, as I was afraid it might. She merely nodded. "Yes. They were together for a long time. I thought they were engaged, but Derek said that was only Darla's idea."

"I see. Did Darla meet him before she came up to London?"

"Yes. She started going out with him in Morbridge. Then he came up here to London, and that's when Darla came too."

"To be near him?"

"Yes."

"That was in October of last year, wasn't it? And you came in November, didn't you? Can you tell me why you came to London, Harriet? Was it because of your friendship with Darla?"

Her answer surprised me. "No. I came to look for my mother!"

"Your mother?"

"Yes. You see, Granny would never talk to me about her. She hated her because she left my father, but I remember her. I was seven years old when she went away, and I know she loved me. She wanted to have me come to live with her and the man she was with, but my father wouldn't hear of it. He hated her too. We were living here in London when it happened, and I always planned that when I was old enough to earn my living, I would come and look for her."

Harriet reached into her shoulder bag and dug out a snapshot in a plastic frame. "Look, here she is. It's the only picture I have."

The snap showed a tall woman with thick dark hair, holding the hand of a small girl, recognizably Harriet. I had expected a young face, but this woman looked to me to be past forty. There was something vaguely familiar about her, but whatever it was eluded me.

I remembered the bit of unfinished embroidery in Harriet's room in Morbridge, the letters "MO" begun and laid aside. "Have you had any luck in tracing your mother, Harriet?"

"No. I talked to a man at a detective agency. He said he could help me but it would cost a great deal of money. I've been saving a bit as I can, but it will take a long time to save enough. I hoped Darla would advise me, as she was so clever, but she said if my Mum was anything like hers, I'd be better off without her."

I smiled encouragingly. "I suspect you saw more of Darla than you told your grandmother?"

I got a watery smile back. "Yes. Granny thought she was a bad influence on me, so I didn't tell her. Actually, at first I did see Darla only now and then, but after a while, we got to be more like real friends, if you know what I mean. We'd talk about Morbridge and all, and she talked about Derek and how she was mad about him, but she always made me promise never to tell anyone his name."

"Why all the secrecy?"

"At first Darla thought he was married and didn't want his wife to know about her, but then she learned that wasn't true. Sometimes he used different names instead of 'Malone,' and she thought he was in trouble with the police, but he never said."

"Hadn't Derek been a prison officer at Princetown before he came to London?"

"Yes, that's where Darla met him, at a party out there."

"Do you know why he left there?"

"He said it was dull work and he thought he could do better on his own."

"And what kind of work does he do in London?"

Harriet frowned and gave me a less than frank look. "He won't say what he does, but he always has money in his pocket."

Even Harriet, I could see, had put that one together. Sooner or later, I thought, Derek would slip up in whatever he was doing, and he might be seeing Princetown from the other side of the bars.

I steered her back to the London scene. "Did you see Derek and Darla together often?"

"Not at first, but a few months ago, we started going about together, the three of us. They were always having rows, and Darla would ring me up or come to my place, sobbing and swearing she'd never see him again. Then he'd turn up and they'd be like lovebirds again. She said he was kinder to her when I was there, and he seemed to like me too."

I refilled our cups and leaned back in my chair. Harriet seemed more relaxed now, and I hoped she'd be ready soon to come clean with whatever was bothering her.

Groping my way, I said, "It must have been sad for you when Darla died."

Harriet's reaction was swift and startling. Tears sprang from her eyes and she tried to wipe them away with the back of her hand. "That's what I wanted to tell you, Mrs. Camden. It was all my fault!"

I stared at the girl. "How can that be?"

"I gave her the pills that killed her! Now do you see why I can't go to the police?"

24

I GOT UP AND PUT MY ARM AROUND HARRIET, AS SHE SAT AT my kitchen table sobbing. "It's all right, my dear, tell me about it and we'll see if we can sort it out."

She gulped out her thanks and fished in her handbag for a tissue as I went back to my chair.

I leaned forward. "Harriet, how could you have given Darla cyanide?"

"Oh, it wasn't cyanide I took. At least I didn't think so. It was ergotamine."

"But didn't you know she died of cyanide poisoning?"

"That's what the police said, but Derek told me sometimes they tell the wrong information so the real criminal is misled."

Was this girl really that naive? Yes, I could see she believed this and probably Derek did too. "Well, Harriet, I can set your mind at rest about that. I attended the inquest on Darla and the doctor who did the postmortem examination definitely said the cause of death was cyanide."

"I know. When we saw that in the news, Derek said maybe I took the wrong thing and what I gave her really was cyanide."

"Maybe you better start from the beginning and tell me what happened."

"Right. It was back in April when Darla told me she was pregnant. She was very excited and said now Derek would surely marry her, but when she told him, he blew his top and said no way. He wasn't ready to have a kid, and so on. About a week later, we were all out having a meal, and Derek told Darla she'd best get on with it—meaning, have an abortion.

"She said she was afraid to have an operation, but I knew she was just stalling, hoping he'd change his mind. Then she said maybe she could take something, like what was that stuff women used to take? I said, 'Ergotamine?' because I had heard some woman talking to the chemist about it at work one day. Darla said that sounded like it. I said the chemist told the woman it's used mainly after childbirth to promote contractions, or something like that, and one needed a doctor's prescription.

"Darla said, 'Then I can't get any,' and Derek said, 'Harriet, you could get it for her.' I was really upset, because I knew what he meant, that I should steal it, and I said I could never do it, but he kept after me and made me promise I would at least try.

"Sometimes I did help behind the counter when they were busy, and the next day, while I was in the back, I looked along the shelves and saw a large container labelled 'Ergotamine.' Now that I knew where it was, I waited till no one was looking. Then I went back later and opened the jar and took out a big handful of pills and dropped them in my pocket. I'm certain that was what the jar said, but I was so nervous, I suppose I might have got the wrong one."

I wondered if pharmacies stocked anything like cyanide in pill form, but I decided I'd better check it out before saying any more to Harriet. Instead, I asked if she knew when Darla took the pills, whatever they were.

"No. She promised Derek she would take them soon. She was going down to Morbridge on Saturday, and she said she would take them there. She'd be staying at home, so if she felt sick, she wouldn't be alone."

"And you never saw her again?"

"No. I usually waited for Darla to ring me if she wanted to get together, so I didn't know she hadn't come back to London until a few days later. That's when Derek came by my place and told me he thought Darla had split."

"Why did he think that?"

"He told me they'd had a flaming row the night before she left. She told him she was sick of the way he treated her and there was someone at home who'd always fancied her. She said she'd take the pills and get rid of his brat, and if this man still wanted her, she'd stay around till he sorted things out."

"What things?"

"That's what I asked, and he said maybe the bloke was married, for all he knew. So, when Darla didn't come back to London, that's when Derek thought she'd done what she said. He rang up the office where she worked and they said she'd called in sick. Then Derek told me he was glad in a way, because Darla had been getting on his nerves and he liked being with a nice quiet girl like me."

I glanced at Harriet and saw just such a look of pleased surprise as she must have exhibited when Derek first said these words to her.

Now her voice became more animated. "He started

coming on to me after that. At first I wondered if he was just planning to make Darla jealous, if she came back and found us together, but pretty soon I believed he really liked me. I had had a few dates with a fellow I met at the chemist's, but Derek was the first—"

She broke off, a flood of color giving an attractive glow to her pale face.

"Your first real boyfriend?"

"Yes. He began staying over at my place sometimes."

"At your room in Trefford Place?"

"Yes. How did you know? Oh, I remember, you said Granny asked you to look for me."

"Did you wonder what had happened to Darla?"

"Oh, yes. After a couple of weeks, I thought about ringing up her family in Morbridge to ask after her, but I knew she'd be furious if I did that, so I just waited. I thought when she was ready, she would get in touch and let me know where she was. Besides, I felt guilty about being with Derek. I guessed it wouldn't last if Darla came back. She was so pretty, and after all, she and Derek had been together for a long time, even through all their rows. Then I knew she would never forgive me for taking up with him."

I thought about all this while Harriet worked on her third cup of tea and some more wafers.

One thing didn't make sense. "Harriet, why did you quit your job and move out of Trefford Place and not write to your grandmother or tell her where you were living?"

Now that haunted look came back to her face. "Don't you see, I had stolen the pills from the chemist's, and as soon as they saw the pills were missing, I knew they would catch up with me and I would go to prison. Derek said it was a very serious offense and he was sorry he'd asked me to do it. They would know I was the one, as the only people who ordinarily work behind the counter are the chemist himself and an old lady in her forties who's been there for centuries."

I smiled inwardly at the "old lady," remembering how ancient the forties had seemed to me when I was eighteen. So, Neil's guess that Harriet had pinched something was confirmed, but not in the way we expected.

Now Harriet went on, "I know I can trust you, Mrs. Camden. You won't tell the police about this, will you?"

I hedged. "I don't think it will be necessary to mention it now, Harriet, but even if it were, I believe they would be more lenient than you think."

This was small potatoes, anyway, I thought, compared to the nitty-gritty of Darla's death from cyanide. Now I asked, "Where did you go when you moved out of Trefford Place?"

"I moved in with Derek. He had a large bedsit in Kilburn then. He moved about fairly often."

Kilburn. Nowhere near the grim room I'd seen in Orcutt Street. That must have come later.

"Did you take another job then?"

"No, Derek said they would find me through the registry if I did."

"Weren't you in need of money?"

"Derek said he had plenty for both of us."

Pretty generous, I thought, compared with the way he had treated Darla. Evidently a placid, undemanding girl like Harriet suited him better than the mercurial Darla, for all her charms.

"When did you first learn what happened to Darla?"

"We were watching the telly and saw the report of a girl's body being found near Morbridge. They showed a picture of her clothing and said she had been dead 'for some time,' but didn't say how long. I said it looked like Darla's striped blouse, the one she liked so much, and Derek said yes it did. Then, when they knew it was Darla, that's when we thought she might have taken the pills I gave her and maybe had fallen into the bog somehow. I cried and cried when I knew she was dead. She was my very best friend."

Harriet wiped a tear away and went on. "It was after the inquest we found out it was cyanide poisoning she died of. You see, I *might* have taken the pills from the wrong jar. Lots of those drugs have weird names that don't sound like what we usually call them. The one that said 'Ergotamine' had some other name too, and it was on a shelf in a row of jars that looked alike."

"But Harriet, didn't you wonder if someone else, someone down in Morbridge, had murdered Darla?"

"I thought about that, but it seemed like they would have hit her over the head or shot her with a pistol or something more ordinary. Derek said cyanide was hard to come by, and that's why he was afraid I had given it to her by mistake. Poor Darla! I still can't believe it all happened."

I decided now was the time to mention my discovery at the registry office that afternoon. When I told the girl I had seen the notice of her intended marriage to Derek, she smiled shyly.

"Yes, we were married last Thursday! Derek said he'd like to marry me if I promised not to have any kids, and I said I didn't want any either. Now that Darla's gone, it seemed all right to marry him." Proudly, she displayed the gold band on her finger.

I noticed Derek hadn't wasted much time getting on with the marriage. "You and Derek listed your address as Orcutt Street. Have you lived there long?"

"Oh, we didn't really live there. Derek knows the

man who lives at that address and paid him something to say that was our address, because you have to establish residence in the borough before you can apply for the certificate."

Casually, I said, "Then you're still living in Kilburn?"

Now she clammed up for the first time in all this confessional outburst.

"No, we moved from there."

I could see she wasn't about to tell me where they *were* living. Derek seemed to have his lady friends well trained in secrecy.

Now I tried to persuade her to tell her story to the police. "Really, Harriet, what you have told me doesn't mean you killed Darla, even accidentally. It's true you took some pills from the chemist's, but you thought you were helping your friend. It was wrong to do that, but the police will look at all the facts and I'm sure they would be fair. As for the robbery, I was there and I can support you."

She hesitated and I pressed on.

"Why don't we go together right now? The police are already looking for you. It will be to your credit to go on your own initiative, don't you see? I'll take you in to the Holborn station myself and stay with you. Shall we do that?"

I could see her longing to say yes, to be relieved of the burden that was haunting her, whatever the outcome.

At that auspicious moment, my doorbell rang.

Pressing the intercom, I heard a young man's voice. "Mrs. Camden? Derek Malone here. I believe my wife is there. May I come up?"

25

THE DEREK MALONE WHO CAME INTO MY FLAT WAS A FAR cry from the rude young man who had tried to bar my way at the Hayward Gallery. Pulling his cap from his tightly-curled head, he held out a courteous hand.

"Mrs. Camden? Derek Malone."

I shook his hand briefly but did not ask him to sit down.

He walked swiftly over to Harriet, where she stood looking as if she expected to be reprimanded. Instead, he put his arm around her. "Hello, luv. I thought you might be here."

Relieved but puzzled, Harriet said, "How did you know?"

Derek looked at me with the smile of a man whose sex appeal has never failed him yet. It failed with me, but I don't think he noticed.

"How did I know? I've heard all about 'wonderful Mrs. Camden' for days!"

I didn't smile back. "How did either of you know my address? It's not listed in the directory."

Harriet gave a sort of gasp and looked helplessly at Derek, who said smoothly, "You got it from your granny, didn't you, luv?"

Harriet blinked. "Oh, yes, of course. From Granny."

Okay, her granny did have my address, although I didn't see why she would have given it to Harriet during their brief ten minutes or so together that night at Morbridge. Oh, well, no matter.

Now Derek got down to business. "Having a good chat, were you?" he asked, with what he no doubt regarded as great subtlety.

Harriet nodded, turning her eyes to me pleadingly. I said, "Harriet came to ask me if I could help clear her of suspicion in the robbery of her grandmother."

Derek looked immensely relieved. "And can you do that, Mrs. Camden?"

"I've already told the police I thought it unlikely Harriet took the money, but of course I have no proof."

Derek gave me a flattering smile. "Still, the word of a lady like you would go a long way, I should think."

The three of us were still standing in the sitting room. Derek's eyes flicked around the room but I made no offer of a chair. Instead, I said severely, "I strongly suggest that Harriet should go to the police of her own accord. They will find her soon enough in any case, and it will be to her credit to go to them first. If she has done nothing wrong, they will have no reason to hold her."

Harriet gave me a grateful look that said thank you for not telling Derek she had confessed to taking the pills from the chemist's.

Derek nodded solemnly. "I'm sure you're right, Mrs. Camden. We'll say goodbye, then. Thanks for your help."

He shook my hand again and swept Harriet toward the door. She turned back and murmured a 'Thank you' as they went toward the stairs.

I hadn't seen much point in telling Derek that I knew about Harriet and the theft of the pills. It would only have made it even less likely he would let her turn herself in to the police. What I needed first was some information.

I went to the phone and rang up the local chemist's I used for my own prescriptions. After a few minutes' wait, the chemist picked up the phone. To my question, he said he stocked nothing that contained sodium cyanide, nor any other form of cyanide, and he thought it unlikely that any chemist would do so.

I thanked him and took out the business directory for central London. By this time, Neil's officers would have located the shop in Queensway where Harriet had worked, but I needn't bother him now to ask for the number. He would be calling me later in the evening. Time enough then to give him the latest.

There were two chemist's shops whose addresses seemed likely, and I tried them both. In each case, I said I was a writer of crime novels and needed information. One man was brusque but willing to say he never stocked cyanide. The other was chatty, confirming that he carried nothing of that nature but suggesting the name of a large chemical firm that dealt in such products. A sampling of three dispensaries certainly was not conclusive, but I thought it sounded pretty unlikely that your average shop carried any cyanide.

I tried the number of the chemical firm, and after some shunting about, spoke to a friendly young man who seemed willing to help. I asked if cyanide ever came in capsule or pill form, and he said, not to his knowledge. It was usually packed in airtight containers and was used chiefly in farming or in scientific laboratories.

By this time I felt reasonably confident that Harriet hadn't mistaken ergotamine for anything containing cyanide. In that case, I could tell Neil the whole story without feeling I had betrayed the girl's confidence. Whoever gave Darla the cyanide, I was pretty sure it wasn't Harriet Thorne. Now I wished I had made those calls while Harriet was still there, but at that time I didn't know what the answer would be. It would have made matters worse if all the chemist's shops had proved to be bursting with jars of cyanide tablets. If only I knew where the girl was staying, I could reassure her and then maybe she would go to the police.

Harriet had been pretty flustered when I asked them how they knew my address. Derek covered it quickly, but I doubted she had got it from her grandmother. How else could they get it? Of course. The night at the Hayward Gallery, when I followed Harriet onto the Hungerford Bridge, my attacker was no stranger. I'd be willing to bet it was Derek. The witnesses described him as young and wearing a cap, so his curly hair would have been covered. He wanted to find out who I was, and in my billfold was my driver's license with my address. The fifty pounds in cash was a nice little bonus. No way to prove it, of course, but I was sure I was right.

With a shrug, I decided to get back to work and picked up my copy of *The Specimen* at the point where Annette had described the night she had spent at Probis Hall. As the journal went on, it was obvious that it took a while before she fully realized she had been betrayed by Sir Wilfred.

The next few entries after the fatal night revealed her surprise that her lover had not come at once to ask

Mr. Spalding for her hand in marriage. It was four days later that the blow fell:

16 June. *I cannot believe it! Uncle tells me Sir W. has gone away on business for a month or more! I asked if he had left a message for me, and Uncle said carelessly, 'Yes, he said to tell you goodbye, as he was rushed and had no time to write. Can't see why he needed to write, but there it is.' There must be something dreadfully wrong. Perhaps he was called away on a personal matter and did not wish to tell Uncle about it. Surely he will write to me soon. . . .*

25 June. *I have waited for the post each day and still no message from Sir W.*

12 July. *It is time for Emily to come home, and still no word from Sir W. I must face the truth at last. He did not care for me, as I believed.*

2 August. *I have been unable to write here in my journal since I knew the truth about Sir W. It has been wonderful having my dear Emily near me, but it is sad to see the fondness grow between her and Stephen Ward, knowing that nothing can come of it but heartache and sorrow.*

4 August. *Sir Wilfred is back! He came to tea this afternoon and behaved toward me as if nothing had happened between us! I wonder if I am going mad? As he was taking his leave, I followed him and asked him to speak to me, but he simply smiled in a friendly way and mounted his horse and rode away.*

12 August. *The thing I have feared so desperately has come to pass. I am very sure that I am with child. Now he* must *marry me. He is after all an honourable man. When I tell him, he cannot refuse! Now I must find a safer place to hide this*

journal, so that my secret cannot be revealed before the matter is settled.

13 August. *A dreadful thing has happened! Sir W. has asked Emily to marry him and he has given her a ring! I ought to have told him sooner of my condition, but I wanted to be sure before I did so. I have sent a note asking him to come to me.*

Evening. *At last he has answered my note and will meet me in the Italian garden tomorrow morning.*

14 August. *I cannot believe Sir Wilfred's duplicity! When we met in the garden just now and I told him about my condition, he raised his eyebrows and asked what this had to do with him. Painfully, I reminded him of the night I spent at the Hall, and he said he had no clear recollection of that night, as he had been drinking a great deal of wine. I pointed out that my condition was proof in itself of my story, and he said that another man may equally have been responsible for that circumstance. 'What about the man Travis?' he asked me. 'I understand he has made you an offer. It might be the best thing for you to accept him.'*

In that moment, all the love I had felt for him turned to a burning hatred. I said that I would go straight to Uncle and tell him the truth.

At first he said no one would believe me, that it was my word against his. Then quite suddenly he became conciliatory. He begged me to wait until tomorrow morning, saying that if he had indeed been responsible, he would of course do the correct thing. We are to meet by the lake at six o'clock tomorrow morning. He will put his affairs in order and make arrangements for me to go to a little village in the south of France, where he will join me later and we will be married.

I longed to tell him how despicable he was and that I would rather die than be married to such a man, but I must think of my unborn child. The world is harsh enough as it is. To be born out of wedlock would be a burden I cannot place upon my innocent child.

And there Annette's journal ended. Emily read again with horror the words that confirmed Sir Wilfred's guilt:

"We are to meet by the lake at six o'clock tomorrow morning."

Instead of sending for Inspector Vickers, Emily put the journal into her reticule and walked briskly to the village, to deliver the evidence to him with her own hands.

I put down the novel, musing about Talbot's handling of the social implications of the tragedy. The significant phrase in Sir Wilfred's rejection of Annette was his statement that no one would believe her, a defense as valid today as it was in the mid-Victorian period. A man of good family, in a position of power, can still deny the act of rape and get away with it. Sir Wilfred would have had no problem convincing George Spalding that Annette was inventing the whole story. His dilemma was that *Emily* would never have bought his denial, and he knew it. If he had any hope of marrying Emily, he had to dispose of Annette before the truth was revealed. He was confident that Annette had not as yet confided in her cousin, as she would try to conceal the terrible disgrace of her pregnancy as long as possible.

Annette Spalding was murdered to avoid scandal. The common motives of lust and greed, love and money, are still around today, but in a society where anything goes, scandal is more often a matter for civil suit than for mayhem.

Or is it?

Stella Bascomb had paid off a blackmailer to save Oliver from scandal. As the Good Book says, there's nothing new under the sun.

26

REMEMBERING IT WAS TIME FOR DINNER, I WENT TO THE kitchen and tossed up a salad while a divine steak I'd picked up from my local butcher sizzled under the grill. With my tray and a glass of Beaujolais in front of the television, I watched the news and part of a dreadful quiz show, waiting for Neil to phone.

But when the phone did ring, it wasn't Neil but Sally.

"Mums, I'm at Beebee's. There's a big problem here and I want to know what you think."

My heart did a swoop. In a flash I reverted from sleuth to basic mother. "What is it, darling?"

"It's Ruby Brown. She rang up Jason at the university and asked him if I would come to Morbridge and help her."

Huge selfish breath of relief. Sally was OK.

"What happened, dear?"

"It's Ruby's father. He tried to—that is—he came into her bedroom and—"

"Molested her?"

"Yes!"

"Oh, poor child. What did she do?"

"She ran to Jason's mother's place, but she didn't want to tell Mrs. Trask what it was all about because she was too ashamed. That's when she rang up Jason and asked me to come."

"And you're at Bea's place now?"

"Yes, I whizzed over to Morbridge and picked up Ruby and brought her here. Beebee left us tons of food and went off to a meeting."

Gradually, the story emerged. Ruby, already fourteen, had only recently started her menstrual periods. Her breasts were developing but not showing under her clothes, and one day Mrs. Brown made a disparaging remark about Darla needing a bra when she was only thirteen. The father smiled at Ruby and said, "That'll do, Leola. Ruby's growing into a fine-looking lass." He gave her a light squeeze on the bottom, and Ruby was so pleased at his admiration, she thought nothing of his gesture.

Recently, her father had gone in for a lot of coarse teasing, but it was such a welcome change from snarls and beatings that Ruby was beguiled into hoping he was becoming fond of her.

"This evening," Sally went on, "both the parents came home from work and they had their 'tea.' That's supper, you know. Then the little brother went out with a friend and Mrs. Brown went to a neighbor's house for a chat. Ruby took her bath and was in her dressing gown in her bedroom when her father came in and started running his hands down her body. He had been drinking and was acting amorous, saying she was his little lady friend, and they could have a good time together.

"At first, she was sort of mesmerized, I gather. He

had closed the door, and now he pressed her onto the bed and said, 'Let's cuddle up together.'"

Sally was no prude, but it was painful for her to describe what happened next. The gist of Ruby's story, I gathered, was that at first she didn't protest, until her father starting putting his hands where they ought not to be. She told him to stop, but he just went on, sort of crooning that she would soon learn to like it. Then she screamed and told him again to stop it, and they heard the young brother's voice calling, "What's up, Ruby?"

Her father leaped off the bed and bent over her. "Not a word of this, mind, or you'll be sorry!"

He opened the bedroom door and said casually to his son, "Ruby had a fall but she's all right now."

Poor Ruby cowered in her room, weeping and shaking, until she heard her mother come in. Shortly afterward, her father went off to the pub, and Ruby took her mother into her room and told her what had happened. To her horror, Leola Brown slapped her hard across the face, snarling, "You little slut. He'd never do that if you didn't lead him on. You girls are all the same. You'll go after anything in trousers." Her voice rose and she screamed at Ruby, "I don't want to hear any more of this, do you hear?"

Sally was tearful as she went on with the story. "That's when Ruby threw on some clothes and ran to Mrs. Trask's house, but once there, she couldn't face talking about it. She didn't want to tell Jason, either— too embarrassing. That's when she thought of me. I asked Ruby if I could get your advice and she said, 'Oh, yes, ask your mother.' So now, Mums, what shall we do?"

Needless to say, I had been thinking about this since the beginning of the story. I said, "It's obvious Ruby ought to go to the police, but I can understand the problems that entails. An alternative would be to go home and threaten both parents with immediate exposure if this ever happens again. Against that is Ruby's own nature. She's not a strong-willed girl. Quite the contrary, she's easily intimidated. I believe they could make her life a misery if she tried that."

Sally said, "Yes, I'm afraid so."

"Have you asked her if she's willing to report the incident?"

"That's what she wants to know from you, whether she should do it or not."

"If she does report it, they'll talk to the parents, who will deny everything. Then, if they send her back home, I'm afraid the father will do exactly as he threatened and beat her unmercifully. If, on the other hand, the police do believe her story, as I think they will, she will surely be put into care."

"You mean a foster home?"

"Yes. You'll need to ask Ruby how she feels about that."

"Right. Hold on, I'll be back."

I expected a long wait on the phone, but in two minutes Ruby herself was on the line. "Mrs. Camden? Sally told me what you said about going into care. I might hate it, but anything is better than going back home. If my mum had believed me, it would be different, but she didn't. I'll tell the police if you think I ought to."

I expressed my sympathy to Ruby and we talked for a bit longer, leaving it that Ruby would call the local Morbridge station, with Sally standing by for support, and I would also report the matter to Superintendent Padgett.

When I hung up, I felt sickened with disgust at the Floyd Browns of this world, exploiting the vulnerable children who should look to them for protection. But what about the mother? She was equally revolting, with her instant defense of the man. Did Ruby look like the kind of girl who would "ask for it" from anybody, least of all her father? And what did Leola Brown mean by saying "you girls are all alike?" It sounded like a reference to all adolescent girls, but what if it was more specific? You and *Darla* are alike?

That day at the letterbox party, Ruby had told me Darla had started to talk to her about something and then decided it could wait. Wasn't it possible she planned to warn Ruby against the father but thought it was not an immediate danger as Ruby was not yet into puberty?

If Floyd Brown tried it on with Ruby, it was a near certainty he had molested Darla. As a stepdaughter, she was an even more vulnerable target. Darla certainly hated both her parents. Maybe she had gone to her mother and, like Ruby, had been rebuffed.

Now Darla was dead and could never testify against her stepfather.

I wondered if Darla had ever confided in anyone about this. If so, it would help to substantiate Ruby's story.

Then I remembered the scar!

At the inquest, Floyd Brown was asked about marks of identity on Darla's body and reported the scar on her abdomen. He claimed he had brought Darla a bandage at the time she cut herself with the razor, but at the party at Princetown, Ruby told me her father wasn't home that day and wondered why he lied about it.

I thought I could put that one together now. Floyd went to the morgue to make the identification. The face was so hideously swollen and decomposed as to be fairly unrecognizable, but height, weight, hair color, and clothing all made it obvious it was Darla. A pertinent item was the scar on her abdomen, and when Floyd was asked about it, he said confidently it was hers. Later, the dental records confirmed the identification.

At the inquest, when Floyd was asked about the scar, he had to invent a plausible excuse for having seen it. True, some families dash about the house in the altogether, but the Browns didn't fit the pattern of the trendy, upscale types who were candidates for that lifestyle. Floyd Brown had looked uncomfortable, to be sure, but he did his best with the story of the Band-Aid. If he wasn't home that day, when could he have seen that scar, which would have been concealed even by a bikini swimsuit, unless he had been engaging in sex play with Darla?

I suspected that whatever they engaged in may have gone on for a long time. Ruby had said Darla and her stepfather used to be "all cozy" until she turned against him, probably when she was old enough to want relations with boys her own age. He may have tried to force her, and maybe at that point she told her mother and got zapped the way Ruby did.

Pure speculation, of course, but it certainly made sense in the light of what just happened to Ruby.

When the phone rang again, it was Neil. "Hello, love," he began. "Is this the pretty, fair-haired lady that lives on Abbey Road and sounds like an American?"

I laughed. "What on earth—?"

"We picked up the lady with the bicycle, and we've been hearing some wild stories. Something about a daughter and the bitch. Your lady is indeed disturbed, I'm afraid. She was living in the cave at Gray's Quarry, as you reported, but she came along with the officer quietly enough. She would give only her first name—Louisa—but no surname nor former address.

She was clutching a copy of the local newspaper and chanting, 'The Bitch was robbed! Serves her right!'"

My first thought was for Stella. Had there been another robbery?

"What did she mean?"

"The article she brandished about was an account of the robbery of Mabel Thorne."

"Mabel?" Then I remembered the report of the woman out walking her dog who saw my bicycle lady ride up to Mabel's house and peer in the window the night Mabel was robbed.

Louisa. Now my lady at least had a name. The day I first met her at the quarry, she said she had seen me with "the Bitch." I assumed she meant Stella, but she could have seen me going into Mabel's house or taking her to the doctor.

Neil went on, "When we picked up her bicycle and compared the tracks outside the kitchen window of the Thorne house, they matched. She admits to seeing you with someone at the kitchen table drinking tea. There was plenty of time for her to nip up the stairs, take the money, and get away while you were still in the kitchen. Do you remember if you locked the front door when you came into the house?"

"No, I just closed it. I suppose I thought it would automatically lock."

"Interesting. It happens that this door doesn't do that. One must turn the bolt from the inside. So, she *could* simply have walked in the front door. You'd have heard nothing from the kitchen, I'm sure."

"Not in that huge house. What does Louisa say to all this?"

"She denies it absolutely but says she would have done it gladly if she'd known where the money was!"

"Oh, dear."

"Exactly. She won't tell us anything about her

relationship to Mrs. Thorne nor why she dislikes her. Just chuckles gleefully. We also get some wild stories about the American lady in Abbey Road."

"She thinks I live at Bea's place?"

"Evidently. And what's all this about falling into a bog out on Dartmoor and how the beautiful lady oughtn't to be walking in the mist without a whistle and she might have died if our Louisa hadn't come along?"

"Oh, I did trip and fall into a mire one day, and she helped pull me out, but I'm sure it was far from fatal. So what happens with Louisa now?"

"We're turning her over to Social Services. We have no conclusive evidence against her, and she's obviously mentally unstable."

Now Neil paused for a little romantic chitchat before getting back to business. "Still no sign of Harriet Thorne. Where *is* that girl, anyhow?"

Smugly, I said, "Camden Investigations at your service, sir. Harriet was here in my flat this afternoon!"

27

"HARRIET THORNE WAS IN YOUR FLAT?"

Neil's usual cool was close to cracking.

"Yes, dear, and then her husband came to fetch her."

"Husband! Claire, what is all this? Start slowly and tell me everything."

I did. I reported my visit to the registry office and gave him the address in Orcutt Street and Harriet's story that it was a phony address. When I described going there and bearding the alcoholic chap in his den, so to speak, Neil clucked. "My dear one, will you *please* stop this sleuthing and leave the investigating to us?"

My temper flared. "Look, Neil, I'm not a child. Do you want to hear this or not?"

"Yes. Please go on." His voice was solid ice.

I filled him in on Derek and Darla, ending with Harriet's theft of the ergotamine tablets.

"I rang up several chemists," I added, "and learned that they don't carry any pills or capsules containing cyanide. So you see, Harriet couldn't have taken them by mistake."

No thaw in the ice. "I could have told you that myself. We've checked extensively on the availability of cyanide. Now, what other information have you failed to report?"

"Come on, Neil. I'm reporting it now. I knew you were going to phone. If you hadn't, I'd have called you."

"So what's this about a husband?"

"Harriet and Derek were married last week."

"Didn't waste much time, did they?"

"No."

"I don't suppose you could have held Harriet and rung up the police? She *is* wanted for questioning, you know."

"Did you want me to tie her to a chair? She's bigger than I am. I might have lost the fight. Then Derek arrived. Do you think I could take on both of them?"

A pause while we both sulked. Then Neil broke the silence. "Harriet may know more than she's telling about her grandmother keeping cash in the house."

"Could be."

"Also, we located the shop in Queensway where she worked. The chemist was surprised when she rang up and gave immediate notice. Said she was a good steady worker, never gave trouble."

"Did he mention that any pills had been taken?"

"Not a word. You say she described the ergotamine as stored in a large jar. These probably aren't used much. He may never have noticed they were gone."

A pause.

Then Neil said, "Sorry I snapped," and I said, "Me, too," and we both broke up laughing. A good sign, I thought.

When we had settled back to normal, I decided it was time for the sad tale of Ruby Brown and her father. Neil's first reaction was, "The bloody bastard. I'd like to kick him where it hurts."

I added, "Ruby and Sally probably rang up the Morbridge station a short time ago. Will you be informed about it?"

"Yes. My officers will handle it, and I'll get the report in the morning. It's helpful to know you've met the girl and find her story believable."

"What's likely to happen to Ruby?"

"It all takes time, but she won't be sent home, that's certain. There will be a hearing, and eventually, as you thought, she'll be placed in care. It's likely to be a better situation for her here in Devon than in some areas of London, where there's a desperate shortage of good placements. We have some fine people available here."

"Neil, what do you think about my theory that Darla had also been molested?"

"I'd say it's spot-on. It sounds as if the bastard had something going there, all right. If she'd reported him, and he was convicted, he'd have gone down for a good stretch."

"I wonder if she ever threatened to do that?"

Neil pondered. "It makes me wonder, too. The father was reported to be away on one of his runs when Darla was last in Morbridge. She was never seen after midday. As I remember from the report, he came back that evening but claimed he spent some time in a pub before going home. I'd say some follow-up is in order."

We batted things around for a while. Then Neil said gloomily, "I don't know when I can get up to London, Claire. Any chance—?"

I smiled. "Why not? I'll go down to Bea's on Friday. You can ring me there when you're free."

Neil chortled. "To paraphrase Christina Rossetti: 'My heart is like a singing bird,/Because my love will come to me!'"

All day Thursday and through the next morning, I worked diligently on Talbot, and by Friday afternoon, I was ready for a break. Sally had phoned the night before with the good news that the court had released Ruby Brown to the temporary care of Mrs. Trask, the mother of William and Jason. When I told Sally I was coming down to Morbridge again, she said, "Ruby would like to see you, Mums," and I promised to get Mrs. Trask's permission to visit the girl.

I left London at noon to avoid the worst of the outgoing traffic, arrived at Bea's in time for a good chat, and by four o'clock was on my way to Mrs. Trask's house in Rose Lane, where I'd been invited for tea.

On a street of prosperous, semi-detached houses of white stucco, the Trask house, I was glad to note, was on the other side of the town from Abbey Road, so that Ruby would not be in close proximity to the Brown ménage. The woman who opened the door was nothing like the plump, motherly type I had for some reason imagined. Thin and angular, hair swept back in an unbecoming twist, Mrs. Trask spoke sharply. "Mrs. Camden? Come in, please."

She led the way to a large sitting room. "Please sit down. I'll just bring the tea. Ruby will be coming from school presently, and I believe your daughter is kindly giving Jason a lift home for the weekend."

The room, with its gold plush sofa and heavy pieces of dark wood, looked coldly formal. Only used for state occasions, I thought.

In a few minutes, Mrs. Trask rolled in a gorgeous rosewood tea trolley, the silver service gleaming, the fragile china undoubtedly the Sunday best. She poured our tea, and we covered the weather extensively.

Mrs. Trask began with, "A fine day, is it not? For the past two days, we have had heavy rain. Was this true in London as well?"

"No, only a slight drizzle."

"Of course, one does not expect fine weather in the second week of June, does one? Have you lived in England for long, Mrs. Camden?"

"Yes, from time to time for many years."

"Then you are accustomed to our changes in weather?"

"Yes, indeed."

We applied ourselves to a slice of rather good cake for a while, and I hoped we had finished with the weather, but no luck.

"I believe you are from California, Mrs. Camden?"

"Yes."

"You have a great deal of sunshine there, I believe?"

May as well join it, I thought. "Yes, we do. We could do with some of your English rain, as we have severe shortages of water each year."

At last, I heard the front door open, and Ruby appeared in the doorway, carrying her school bookbag.

Mrs. Trask said, "Here you are then, Ruby. When you've put away your things, you may come and join us for tea."

Ruby disappeared up the stairs, and I turned to Mrs. Trask with a smile. "It's very good of you to look after Ruby just now."

No answering smile. "My son suggested that I do so.

Jason has brought Ruby here from time to time. She will be no trouble, I am sure."

When Ruby came in, she said hello to me in a whisper and flushed a deep red, the painful shame of the innocent victim. I felt again that rush of fury toward her father. The situation would be agony to any young girl, and especially so to one as shy as Ruby.

While she drank her tea and applied herself to a generous slice of cake, I asked her about her classes and told one or two amusing anecdotes of Sally's schooldays in California. Anything to avoid the subject that had in fact brought us together.

When Mrs. Trask went to the kitchen for more hot water for the tea, Ruby gave me her timorous smile. "Thank you, Mrs. Camden."

"I didn't do much, Ruby."

Ruby said simply, "You helped me to leave home."

Her next remark surprised me. "Everyone's been so kind to me. Mrs. Trask is wonderful."

Had I missed something in that lady's stony exterior? It soon became clear that I had, for when Sally and Jason came bursting in, full of smiles, Mrs. Trask's formidable visage altered. When I looked at my pretty, vivacious daughter, I felt the familiar surge of maternal pride, and in that moment, I saw Mrs. Trask's eyes light up in the same way as she looked at Jason.

Now the conversation bubbled freely, moving before long to the robbery at Mabel's house and the police search for Harriet. Always glad to work Darla into the conversation, Jason said, "Harriet used to hang about at your place, didn't she, Ruby? She was fond of Darla, and I suspect she went up to London about a month after Darla did, hoping to keep up the friendship."

Exactly what I had thought, till Harriet told me she had gone to London not to be with Darla but to look for her long-lost mother.

Sally asked, "Did Mrs. Thorne have a lot of money or was this her life savings that was stolen?"

Mrs. Trask compressed her lips. "I've always heard that Mabel Thorne lived very frugally. I've seen her at the supermarket shopping for items with reduced prices."

Ruby looked up in surprise. "The last time Darla was at home, she told me Mrs. Thorne was a rich lady."

Jason shook his head. "I don't know about that. Harriet never had much allowance. She did babysitting to earn her pocket money, as I recall."

When they had exhausted the subject of the robbery, Jason turned to me and asked about the progress of the opus on Mary Louise Talbot.

"At the moment, I'm working on *The Specimen*."

Jason grinned. "Oh, I adored that novel. Isn't that the one where the fellow murders the pregnant girl in order to marry the one with the money?"

"Yes!"

"What was his name? Sir Wilfred Probis. That creep!"

When Sally and I were ready to leave and started for the door, I saw Ruby give Mrs. Trask an adoring look and ask if she should clear away the tea things.

So much, I reflected, for first impressions.

When I reached Bea's house on Abbey Road, Sally was just parking her Mini in the drive and I pulled up behind her, but instead of getting out of the car, I sat transfixed.

I heard again Jason's summary of Talbot's novel: *"He killed the pregnant girl so he could marry the one with the money."*

Harriet didn't know her grandmother had money, and I didn't believe for a moment she was clever enough to carry off that deception.

But Darla knew! She told Ruby that Mrs. Thorne was a rich lady.

It all added up. No doubt about it.

28

WHEN SALLY AND I WALKED IN THE DOOR, BEA GREETED US with the unhappy news that Mabel Thorne was gravely ill and had been taken to the hospital that afternoon, where Bea had visited and found her barely able to speak. Mabel admitted at last that she had been suffering from cancer for many months but "didn't want to give way to it." Now she hoped to see her granddaughter again "before the end."

Bea added, "Harriet phoned here a few minutes ago, asking for you, Claire. I told her about her granny and she's promised to visit her. I tried to get her to leave a number where you could reach her, but she refused."

Sally said, "I can understand that! The police have been scouring the country for her for days."

Bea nodded. "Exactly. I told her you were expected shortly, Claire, and she'll ring back any time now."

I had just changed into jeans and a sweater when Harriet's call came.

"Mrs. Camden? I'm so glad to find you. I rang your flat in London and got your message machine, so I thought I would try here."

That sounded as if she was in Morbridge. "Where are you, Harriet?"

"If I tell you, will you promise not to call the police until I've talked to you again?"

Since there was nothing I wanted more than to have another chat with Harriet myself, I promised.

"All right, then, I'm at Granny's. If you'll come round to the back, I'll let you in."

Telling Bea and Sally I wasn't sure when I'd be back and to ask Neil to leave a message if he phoned, I put on a light jacket and walked down Abbey Road to the Thorne house, going as directed to the rear door.

As I followed Harriet through a large pantry into the kitchen, I saw that her face was puffed from weeping.

Her voice thick with suppressed tears, she said, "Poor Granny. Mrs. Camden told me."

Politely, she asked if I wanted tea. "Thank you, no. I've just had tea, but have you any sherry?"

I'm not that fond of sherry, but anything alcoholic sounded good at that point, and I doubted if Granny had stocked anything more potent.

With shaking hands, Harriet fished around on a shelf and produced a bottle, pouring the sherry into a couple of wine glasses.

We sat down—where else?—at the kitchen table, and I asked her if Derek was with her.

"He's gone out to get us some food, and he said he had to talk to somebody while he was out."

Now I asked her how I could help.

"I dare not go to the hospital to see Granny, don't you see? Derek simply won't hear of my going to the police, Mrs. Camden. Now he wants to get phony passports for us so we can leave the country. We came down here to get my passport from when I went to France on a school trip. They can change the name so it otherwise looks genuine. I'm so afraid. If they catch us trying to escape, it will be much worse than if I just go to them now, don't you think?"

I could see that Harriet knew she was right about this but she hadn't the strength to stand up to Derek. In her time of crisis, she had come to regard me as the mother figure she'd never had in her life, someone to back her up, help her take a decisive step.

I could do that much for her, but I couldn't spare her the pain of learning the truth about Derek.

At least I could begin with the good news. "Yes, Harriet, I believe you're absolutely right, and I have something to tell you that will make it easier for you. The chemist's where you worked and where you took the ergotamine tablets does not stock anything containing cyanide. So you see, you could not have mistaken the pills and therefore you had nothing to do with Darla's death!"

She did perk up at that. "Oh, Mrs. Camden, I *am* glad. You see, I never did believe I could have taken the wrong thing, but Derek said I must have done, and I was so frightened!"

"So, now, why don't we ring up the police? You'll feel much better to face up to them, I know."

"But what about Granny's money? They still think I took it, or at least I can't prove I didn't. You said yourself you believe me but you don't really know what happened."

I decided it was time. "Harriet, I want to ask you a question, and I want you to tell me the truth. Was Derek here in the house that night?"

She took a deep breath, and her eyes looked back into mine. "I don't think so."

"But he was here in Morbridge with you?"

In a whisper, "Yes. He drove me down."

"Why did you come?"

"I wanted to see Granny, because she was so ill."

"Was Derek in the house when I first saw you coming down the stairs?"

"No. He was across the road in the van, waiting for me."

"Are you sure? You do see that while we were here in the kitchen, Derek might have come into the house and taken the money?"

"How would he know where to look?"

"He wouldn't, but if he found your granny asleep, it's a good bet he'd look in her desk."

Harriet looked stricken but I noticed she didn't protest that Derek would never have done such a thing.

I decided to take another tack. "Harriet, tell me about Derek's van. How long has he had it?"

"For several weeks, I'm sure."

"Did he have it before Darla came down here to Morbridge the last time?"

"Let me think. We went out for a meal the night before she left. Oh, I remember, he had bought the van that day or the one before, and he was boasting about what a good price he paid, considering it had a fresh paint job. As we were leaving, I went out with them to look at it, and I could smell the paint."

"What color is it?"

"Dark blue, almost black."

Okay. I thought, time to get down to it. "Were you surprised when Derek wanted to marry you so soon?"

"Yes, but he told me once we were married, he couldn't testify against me about the pills for Darla."

"You see, it could also be the other way about. If

you were married, he believed *you* couldn't testify against *him*."

"About what?"

I started to answer when a voice called out, "I'm back."

Derek came through the pantry and into the kitchen, carrying a bag. "Mrs. Camden!"

"Hello, Derek. I happened to stop by and found Harriet here." Would he buy that? It didn't matter now whether he did or not. The minute I got back to Bea's, I'd ring up the police.

Derek's eyes bored into mine.

I stood up. "Thank you for the sherry, Harriet. I must be going."

Derek put the bag down on the table. "I bought some take-away, luv. You wait here while I walk out with Mrs. Camden."

"That's not necessary." I walked swiftly toward the back door, with Derek one step behind.

No use trying to shake him. I let him fall in beside me and headed for the drive, giving him a fatuous smile. "I promised Harriet I wouldn't tell the police she's here."

"That's very decent of you."

We turned the corner, near the old carriage house which at some distant time had been converted to a garage, and where masses of thick-leaved trees screened Mabel's house from the view of neighbors. I held out my hand. "Well, then, goodbye, Derek."

In a flash, he stepped behind me and I felt his forearm around my neck. He pulled my body back against his, while agonizing pain in my throat nearly cut off my breathing.

If this was what the police meant by a choke hold, I could see why it worked. I couldn't cry out, I couldn't get free. He pulled me backward, my feet taking stumbling short steps against my will. I tried pulling at his arm to no effect. Derek wasn't a large man, but I could feel the strength in that steely arm.

In seconds, he pulled me through a door and slammed it behind us. We were in the converted garage, and beside us stood a dark-colored van. Derek pulled something out of his pocket, threw me to the floor and sat on my buttocks, pulling my arms to the back. I felt something like cold metal and heard a click. Handcuffs? Of course, he had been a prison officer. There was something practiced about this whole procedure. This must be how they were trained to subdue obstreperous prisoners.

"All right, milady. In here, please."

He pulled me to my feet and opened the back doors of the van, pushing me none too gently into the back.

"Lie down," he ordered, and I did. Now he tied my ankles together, then stepped out and closed the van doors. I could hear the rumble of the big garage doors opening, and in a moment he jumped into the driver's seat and backed out of the drive onto Abbey Road.

I'd like to think I stayed cool and collected, but the truth is, I was sick with terror. If Derek had done what I believed he had done, he wasn't going to be too gentle with me.

It all came together, the speedy marriage to Harriet once Darla was out of the way. Darla knew about Mabel's money because she had worked in Oliver's office. Since Oliver was Mabel's financial adviser, Darla would have seen the extent of Mabel's holdings, and probably also a will in Harriet's favor, and she had chattered to Derek about it.

Darla could also have known that Mabel had cancer. She might have asked the receptionist at the doctor's office, or she could simply have pulled

Mabel's file and read it. I remembered sitting in the reception area next to the tall file cabinet. Anyone could pull a file when the receptionist was out of the room. No point in telling Harriet what she knew. Once Harriet had inherited the money, Darla no doubt hoped to get some fringe benefits from the friendship.

Now I discovered that being bound hand and foot was not only painful but extremely inconvenient. For openers, I couldn't wipe my face. When I had hit the concrete floor of the carriage house, my cheek was painfully grazed. I rolled onto my side and brushed my face awkwardly against the shoulder of my jacket, sickened by the sight of the blood that smeared the fabric.

The foul odors on the carpeted floor of the van added to my nausea. Derek was hardly the type to sprint around using a Dustbuster. It was also hard to brace myself against the bumping floor of the van as we drove. With some effort, I drew up my knees and managed to sit up and lean against the side, but Derek looked back and barked, "Get down!"

I didn't argue.

Soon the bumping of the van increased, and I knew we had left the town and were on a less-traveled road. Out on the moor, of course. Was he planning to dump me in the same place where he had put Darla's body?

How did Derek know about this part of the moor, anyhow? Princetown, where he had worked, was more than twenty miles away. Then I remembered. One of the officers at the party had mentioned taking the fellow Malone out letterboxing a few times and said Derek had found it boring. They might well have come over to the area around Morbridge and High Tor on their excursions.

From where I lay, I could see the side of Derek's

face as he drove. Taking some deep breaths and trying to steady my voice, I attempted sweet reason. "Look, Derek, there's no way I can harm you. I was just having a chat with Harriet—"

He gave me one venomous glance and looked back at the road. We bumped on in silence for a while. Then I felt the van make a left turn onto an even rougher surface, and soon it came to a stop.

Derek hopped out, opened the van doors, and untied my legs, putting the cord in his pocket.

"Out we go."

Awkwardly, without my hands to help me, I scrambled down and nearly fell, as my legs, numb from being tied, failed to support me.

Derek held me up and waited till I got my balance.

I glanced around, and at first I saw only barren moorland in every direction. Then something clicked, and I realized we were not far from the rim of Gray's Quarry, visible only to someone who knew it was there.

"This way," he growled, pulling my arm none too gently and walking me toward the edge of the quarry.

As my legs began to feel secure again, I looked toward the far side of the quarry and gasped. "What's that?" I whispered.

As Derek turned to look, I broke away and started to run. Maybe I could make it to the road and by some miracle a car would come along.

No such luck. I hadn't gone twenty yards when I was tackled from behind and fell ignominiously into a clump of bracken. Better than falling on rocks, I thought.

Now Derek was really angry. He pulled me to my feet and slapped me hard across the face, on the cheek that was already banged up.

"Think you're pretty clever, eh?"

He pulled a revolver out of his jacket. "See this? No use running away. Let's go."

As I was marched back toward the quarry, I said, "I don't understand. If you're going to shoot me, why here?"

"Who says anything about shooting? That's only to keep you from running off. We'll just take you down here to the quarry. It may be some little time before you're found, and that's what I need. Plenty of time."

Oh, Louisa, I moaned to myself. Where are you now that I need you? If only I hadn't told Neil where my dear bicycle lady was hiding out, she might have been here to save me again.

Now we stood at the edge of the quarry, by the path leading down into that fairy grotto.

And then it hit me. There was one chance. I might as well try!

29

I STEPPED BACK FROM THE EDGE OF THE QUARRY AND FACED Derek. "Look, if I could get you twenty thousand pounds in cash, would you make a deal to let someone know where I am after you've got safely away?"

He looked as skeptical as I thought he would. "Another of your tricks, eh?"

"No. Just beyond that rise of ground, out on the moor, there's a container with the money in it. I know, because I put it there myself."

"So, who puts that kind of money in a place like that?"

"That's why I didn't want to tell you at first. The money belongs to an elderly lady who doesn't trust banks, and it's her entire life savings. She had been hiding it in her house, but her neighbor was robbed the other day and the lady is terrified she'll be next. She asked me to hide it for her, and I did."

"What if somebody finds it?"

"Believe me, they won't. I got the idea from the letterboxers, but this is not on their list, so there's no reason for anyone to be looking where I put it. Besides, it's hidden where it can't be seen."

I could see the greed in his eyes, and I went on in a tearful voice. "I wouldn't lie to you now, Derek. Please, please, promise to help me out if I give you the money. I'll pay the lady back even if it takes years. You'll still have plenty of time to get away."

He ran a hand through his mop of tight curls. "May as well have a look."

I had no illusion about what he was thinking. If the money was there, he'd take it and never call anyone. He figured someone would find me sooner or later. The one good sign was that he did buy the story of the old lady, as I thought he would. People were inclined to think old ladies always had cash around anyhow, and the recent example of Mabel dramatically confirmed his belief in my story.

We started off toward the spot where I had put the money for Stella. I knew the blackmailer would have picked it up long ago, undoubtedly also taking the container, which would come in handy for the next round. They never stopped with the first payment, that was certain.

Derek kept one hand on his revolver as we trudged silently along the uneven ground. We went over the rise, and I looked down at the flat rock and the pool. What had Mrs. Trask said in her dissertation on the weather? It had rained heavily for two days, before turning fair today. Good.

"It's here," I said, stepping gingerly onto the rock and kneeling to peer over the side.

With a breath of relief, I saw that no container was visible.

"Where?" Derek looked over my shoulder.

"Down there. It's in a flat tin box. You have to lie on your stomach to get it."

"All right, you get it."

"With my handcuffs on?"

"OK, I'll take them off. But don't try anything, see?"

He took out a small key and released my hands. I brought them together, rubbing them and moaning. "I can't move my fingers," I said in a peevish whine.

"Well, give it a try."

Dutifully, I lay down on the rock and reached over the edge, making a show of groping among the rocks below. "I can't do it," I groaned. "The box is under that sharp-pointed rock, and my hands are too stiff. I can't budge it. You'll have to get it."

Derek frowned. Then he told me to sit down, and taking the cord out of his pocket, he tied my ankles again. He started to put on the handcuffs when I said, "You'll have a better chance of getting the box if I hold your legs. I can't get away as long as you feel my hands. If I let go, you've still got your gun."

He thought that one over and evidently agreed. Under the circumstances, I could hardly be going anywhere.

He stretched out on the rock and reached down, pulling hard at the rock I had indicated. "OK, hold my feet," he ordered.

I got a good grip on his ankles and felt him inch forward till his body was half over the edge, both arms grasping the rock.

Then I knelt down, and using all my strength, I twisted his legs and gave him a mighty heave-ho.

With a thundering splash, he sank into the foul waters of the bog, coming up sputtering and livid with fury. "What the shit!" he shouted at me. "You'll pay for this, you bloody bitch."

Suddenly he stopped, and I saw the look of bafflement on his face as he tried to get his footing.

Desperately, he reached for the edge of the rock. Then he tried for those enticing mounds that were just too far away.

If he'd been a tall man with very long arms, he might have had a chance, but Derek was not more than five foot seven or eight, with arms to match. He could reach several inches closer than I had been able to do, but that wasn't enough.

Now I watched as he struggled to free himself and saw his look of puzzlement turn to horror as he felt the mud pulling his legs down.

"Mrs. Camden!" he shouted. "This joke has gone far enough. This is a goddamn quagmire. You've got to get me out of here."

I sat on the rock and watched him silently. Then I bent over and untied the cord around my ankles.

"Look," he bellowed, "I'm sinking deeper. See that cord in your hand? Hold one end and throw it out to me."

"All right, I'll help you in a minute, but first tell me about Darla. She was pregnant and wanted you to marry her, didn't she?"

"I told her I didn't want kids, but she wouldn't listen."

"It was more than that, wasn't it, Derek? You wanted to marry Harriet and get all that lovely money."

"Sure, why not?"

"So, why didn't you just break it off with Darla and go with Harriet?"

Derek had sunk almost to his shoulders, and now he screamed at me, "Never mind all the talk. You've got to help me. I'm going to drown in this bloody bog."

Serenely, I went on. "I'll tell you one reason why, Derek. Because if you'd left Darla when she was pregnant, or forced her to get an abortion against her will, Harriet would never have taken up with you. She was too fond of Darla for that, wasn't she?

"But I think there was a more important reason. Darla knew too much about your criminal activities. You didn't tell her what was going on, but Darla was clever, and I think she threatened to talk about your connection with the man Hopkins. You met him when he was a prisoner at Princetown. You and Hopkins had a lot of enterprises going. You stole the van with the cyanide in it, and Hopkins painted the van for you. Darla knew enough to make things sticky for you. That's the other reason you killed her, wasn't it?"

He glared at me. "Killed her? What the shit? I didn't kill Darla! I never saw her again after she came down here to Devon."

A likely story, I thought. I'd hardly expected a confession.

I looked at Derek and saw the water had risen to shoulder height but hadn't reached his neck. The level of the pool looked to me to be about the same as on the day of my fateful plunge. The recent heavy rain would have counteracted any lowering from the warmer days before. Derek was three or four inches taller than I, so this should be about where he would hit bottom.

I waited, and sure enough, his protests stopped and a beatific look of relief suffused his face. I knew that feeling. His feet are on solid ground, and he thinks it's all over.

I stepped off the rock and called out a cheery goodbye. "Someone will be along soon to pull you out."

Back at the van, I was relieved to see the keys were in the ignition, and I drove at top speed back to Bea's place and dialed Neil's number.

30

I STAYED IN MORBRIDGE UNTIL I'D FINISHED ANSWERING questions for Neil and his cohorts, signing depositions, and so on. I was enormously relieved that no one had rescued Derek before the police got there. As I sped back to town in his van, I had pictured him being pulled out of the bog by a passing letterboxer, a park ranger, or even by Louisa on her bicycle.

Neil told me they found the prison officer who had taken Derek out letterboxing on several occasions. He confirmed my guess that they had walked over the area where Darla's body was found, and the officer had pointed out the danger of the bog. On another occasion they had explored Gray's Quarry while locating a letterbox there.

A week later, when I was back in London, Derek Malone was still being held on the robbery charge while Neil and his officers looked for specific evidence to tie him to the murder of Darla Brown.

"He denies killing the girl," Neil said, "but one would scarcely expect him to do otherwise."

In London, the man Hopkins admitted it was Derek who brought the van to him to be painted, and the date confirmed Harriet's statement that it was the day before Darla left for Morbridge in April.

"Hopkins is a nasty piece of goods," Neil told me. "He's been in and out of prison for years and knows the ropes. He told us enough to get himself off the hook for the moment. Said the van Malone brought in had some lettering on the side, but of course he didn't notice what it was. Yes, there was a container in the van that was labelled as poison, but Hopkins swears that when his lady friend told him to get rid of it, he dumped the entire contents of the van into a rubbish tip before doing the paint job. He admitted to being in steady contact with Malone but insisted it was just an innocent friendship."

As for Harriet, she knew nothing about Darla's death, but when it came to the theft of her grandmother's money, she admitted she suspected Derek all along but didn't want to face it. She went back to their place in London, broke open a locked suitcase, and found the envelope with most of the money still there. At first she believed that because they were married, she couldn't testify against Derek. She learned soon enough that the rule meant only that she couldn't be forced to do so if she didn't *wish* to.

I wondered if Derek's hold over her was strong enough to keep her silent. Not a chance. When she saw that money, with her grandmother's handwriting on the envelope, she had had it with Derek.

"I've always been afraid of him," she admitted to me. "He would be so kind to me one day and so cold the next. He hit me a couple of times, and then he would beg forgiveness and promise never to do it again, but I knew he had been that way with Darla, and I thought it might get worse after we were married."

"Then why did you marry him, Harriet?" I knew it was a silly question. Creep though he was, Derek was a sexy guy.

Her answer gave my heart a twist. "He kept on telling me he loved me, and no one had said that to me since I was a little girl, before my mother went away."

"That reminds me, Harriet. What is your mother's name?"

"Mother? It's Louisa. Why?"

Harriet was promptly reunited with her mother and in due course was appointed by the court to look after her. Louisa, who had been under a doctor's care in London for several years, was not destitute but had moved into the cave at Gray's Quarry because she liked it there. She had come to Morbridge to try to find her daughter, but when she approached Mabel and was told Mabel didn't know Harriet's address, Louisa naturally thought she was lying, and her hatred grew into an obsession. The night she saw Harriet and me in Mabel's kitchen, she had no idea she was looking at her daughter.

A few days after entering the hospital, Mabel Thorne died, grateful at the end for Harriet's constant attendance in her final days. Now Harriet planned to terminate her marriage to Derek on grounds of fraud, and once her grandmother's estate was settled, she and Louisa would live in comfort.

In the Talbot biography, I finished the discussion of *The Specimen*, noting the classically contrived ending. George Spalding suffered a fatal stroke when Sir Wilfred Probis was carted away by the police, leaving Emily with the money and the freedom to marry

Stephen Ward. A tidy wrap-up, to be sure, but Talbot's readers wanted a happy ending and she gave it to them.

Sally came up to London to spend the weekend with me and catch a little nightlife with her friends. When her term ended in July, Miles and Pierre were taking her to Italy for ten days, and she was thrilled. "We'll drive through some of the hill towns I've never seen!"

I felt a stab sharper than any I'd had since Neil had waltzed into my life, remembering a glorious holiday with Miles years ago. The square towers of San Gimignano, the black-banded duomo in Orvieto, a little café in Gubbio flashed past and glimmered away.

Sally didn't miss much. "You and Daddy?"

"It's truly okay, darling. Neil and I are planning a holiday in Paris when his case is closed. Things balance out, you know."

Sally beamed. "I really like him, Mums. And to think he did English Lit at the university. All this and heaven too!"

When Sally had gone out for the evening, I sat in the summer dusk and thought about Neil. What I hadn't told Sally was that Neil and I had bumped into our first real crisis a few days earlier. He had come up to London on the case and we met for dinner. He seemed moody, and when I pressed him, he snapped that nothing was the matter. I dropped it, and after the meal, we walked along the embankment, where the Thames was muddy-sided at low tide.

When we stopped to lean on the wall and watch the lighted boats moving along, he said, "I'm sorry, Claire. I *am* disturbed and I suppose I hoped it didn't show."

"It's okay. What happened?"

"It's Janice. She came to see me rather late last night. I think she'd been drinking, which she doesn't do all that much. She was sort of weepy and talking about the divorce being a mistake. She didn't quite say let's try again, but she was hinting at that."

"Did you tell her about us?"

A pause. "No."

"You didn't?" I was angry and I didn't try to hide it. We had been together pretty often since early June, on terms not merely of sexual intimacy but of genuine affection. I thought he might at least have mentioned me to his wife.

Neil was immediately defensive. "I told her I'd rather leave things as they were. That ought to suffice."

"Did she leave?" I knew I shouldn't have asked that, but I couldn't stop myself. I was astonished at the scalding pain I felt at the thought of Neil in bed with his own wife, separated or not. I also knew enough about English divorce laws to know that if she had stayed, the whole thing would be off. If they remained apart for two years, the proceedings would go forward, but if they didn't, it could take five years or more.

This is crazy, Claire, I told myself. Why do you care about his divorce, anyhow? You're not looking for marriage.

At my question, Neil stiffened and glared at me. "No, she didn't spend the night, nor any part of the night, if that's what you mean."

"Oh, God, Neil, I'm sorry."

Now I pulled myself together and faced reality. What if, a year or so after we separated, Miles had come back to me and hinted that it was all a mistake and that we might try again. Come on, Claire, I admitted. Would I have said no, I've met someone else? Would I have told him about Neil?

But it's different for Neil, I argued silently. Surely

he didn't care for Janice as I did for Miles. Or did he? He was pretty depressed when we first met. And what was it he said about her when he was telling me about his marriage that night in Torquay? "I thought I had won first prize at the fair."

In the end, we made it up, but the result of the whole episode was curious. Neil obviously saw my reaction and seemed to find it reassuring. For me, it made me pull back ever so slightly. As I had said to Sally in another context, things balance out.

Now, as I sat musing, the phone rang and I felt the old familiar rush of pleasure at the sound of Neil's voice.

"Claire? A new development. A witness has come forward with a pretty strong motive for Oliver Bascomb to put Darla Brown out of the way. You know these people well. I'll want your opinion!"

31

STUNNED AT NEIL'S NEWS, I ASKED, "WHAT HAPPENED?"

"A young P.C. in Morbridge was out with his girlfriend, and she mentioned a rumor she had heard concerning Oliver Bascomb and Darla Brown. When pressed, she gave him the name of the friend who had told her the tale, and that friend in turn named the receptionist in Bascomb's office as the source of the story."

"A pretty young woman named Betty Drake?"

"Yes."

"I've seen her in Oliver's office."

"Right. She began by denying everything, but after persistent questioning, she broke into floods of tears and admitted she had spied on her boss. She's obviously enamored. Her story is that in February, when Darla came to Morbridge, she heard her on the phone to Oliver asking him to meet her for lunch. Betty seems to have been wildly jealous of Darla, suspecting there had been some hanky-panky between them before Darla went to London.

"On the day of Darla's call, Oliver left the office shortly before one o'clock, and Betty got into her own car and followed him. He picked up Darla at that cul-de-sac on the road that leads to Becky Falls and drove on up to the falls, where he and Darla ate some sandwiches. Then they started kissing, and one thing led to another, so to speak. Our witness, afraid to be seen, drove away and waited at the cul-de-sac. It was some time later when Oliver dropped Darla back where he had picked her up."

I gulped. Now it was clear that Betty was the blackmailer. Would she confess to this, too? If so, I was in big trouble. The whole story of my leaving the money would come out, and I couldn't see Neil taking a very friendly view of my silence about it.

I kept my voice steady. "So Oliver was having an affair with Darla. How does that connect to her murder?"

"February, dear one. Darla's child was obviously conceived around that time. Now comes the next revelation of our Betty. In April, on Darla's last visit to Morbridge, she came into the office while the clerk was out and only Betty was there. She was closeted with Oliver in his office for at least half an hour, and as the door opened for her to leave, Betty heard her say, 'Till later, then.' Darla was never seen again, so far as we know, except by the killer. Bascomb's motive is pretty clear. She tells him she's pregnant, saying nothing about a boyfriend in London. Maybe she wants money to keep quiet. Maybe she wants him to divorce his wife and marry her. In any case, he's afraid he *could* be the father, or even if he isn't, the scandal would finish his political ambitions."

"Why didn't Betty come forward about this before?"

"Evidently she didn't want to hurt him, and I'd guess she had hopes of being Darla's replacement as girlfriend. She's still never thought of Bascomb as murderer, only as a lothario, and we didn't suggest otherwise to her."

Relief flooded over me. Betty may have broken down to the police, but apparently she had enough sense of self-preservation not to admit to blackmail.

I asked, "Have you talked to Oliver yet?"

"No. We're talking first to everyone around him, hoping to get something specific. You've known him for some years, I take it. What is your opinion?"

I thought that one over. "I don't know, Neil. It's hard to imagine a personal friend as a murderer, but I know it happens all the time. I think you're right about the motive. Oliver does care terribly about the election prospects."

"Right. I scarcely expect you to say more than that. Thank you, darling. I'll keep you posted."

When I put down the phone, I thought back to the day I was reading *The Specimen* and reflecting on scandal as a motive for murder. Like Sir Wilfred, Oliver faced disaster if a young woman's pregnancy was revealed. To protect Oliver from scandal, Stella had paid the blackmail, fearing, as I thought, that he might be the father of Darla's child. Had she, in fact, had a deeper fear? Had she suspected that he might have killed Darla?

Thinking of Oliver Bascomb as a cold-blooded murderer took some effort of imagination until I remembered how desperately he wanted that seat in Parliament. Macbeth was probably a perfectly charming guy until his vaulting ambition o'erleaped itself. The bog where Darla Brown's body was found wasn't on Oliver's land, but he had grown up on the moor and knew the whole area like the back of his hand.

But where would a Morbridge solicitor get hold of cyanide?

The answer was only too obvious. The Bascombs were landowners. I remembered riding Bea's bicycle out to visit Stella and stopping in the large shed below the house to put on my jacket against the rain. Did any of those supplies on the shelves contain sodium cyanide? Neil and his cohorts would be onto that one like a shot.

Two days later, I was back in Morbridge, having been summoned by a shattered and desperate Stella. Oliver had been taken in for questioning in connection with the murder of Darla Brown.

At Herons, where I found Stella numb with shock, I said, "He's not actually charged, is he?"

Stella's voice shook. "Not yet, but it seems to be only a matter of time."

She had been told about the evidence of Betty Drake. "That rotten little bitch. Blackmailing me! At least, she hasn't confessed to that."

"I'm glad to hear it. Anyway, Stella, the police may see a motive for Oliver, but have they any specific evidence against him?"

The black eyes bored into mine. "Why do you think I sent for you, Claire? That's what I want you to find out for me. You can surely get your superintendent to tell you what's going on."

It wasn't the first time I'd been fed up with Stella's arrogance. In her view, the world existed to serve people like the Bascombs. She'd used me once. I wasn't about to be her patsy again. I gave her a straight look. "That's impossible, Stella. Just forget it."

A flash of anger, then a patronizing smile. "It must be love, to garner such loyalty."

No use trying to explain moral principles to Stella. I pointed out that any evidence the police possessed would be made available to Oliver's solicitor, if it came to that.

She said, "Yes, but I want to know *now!*"

Why now? I looked at her curiously. Something in her whole demeanor puzzled me. I decided to lay it on the line.

"Stella, I know how much his political career means to Oliver. Do you really believe he's innocent?"

She looked at me aghast. "Of course he's innocent! You know Oliver. He'd never do a thing like that!"

If I'd expected hesitation or doubt, I certainly didn't get it.

We talked round and round a while longer, and at last I left her in the hands of a local friend who arrived to take over as dispenser of moral support.

That evening, at Neil's place, I assured him I would divulge nothing to Stella, and he filled me in on the current status of the case. It seems his officers had questioned everyone even remotely connected with the Bascombs and had come up with a witness who placed Darla near Herons on the afternoon of the day she was last seen.

Neil said, "This chap is a sort of foreman for the workers on the Bascomb farms, and on that day, he came up to get something from a shed below the house where supplies are stored. And incidentally, in that shed, on a shelf, our lads found a large tin of sodium cyanide. The foreman fellow came back down the hill and was surprised to see an attractive young woman walking up the road toward the house. The time was perhaps two to three o'clock in the afternoon, but he couldn't make it closer than that."

"I presume he identified her as Darla?"

"Yes. No doubt on that score."

"So where has he been all this time when the media begged for news of her?"

"It seems he's a bachelor in his sixties, has no telly, and seldom reads the news except for the sports. He only remembers the date because he had that day been called up to Cumbria to visit his elderly mother, who was dying in a cottage hospital in their native village. She lingered on for a week or so, and he stayed on with his sister till after the funeral. When questioned and shown a picture of Darla, he was perfectly clear about what he had seen."

"So, Darla was there. Do you know where Oliver was?"

"According to his office appointments, he saw a client at half-past one, but there's no record of his time after that."

"What does Oliver say?"

"He admits to seeing Darla in his office but insists he stayed on the rest of the afternoon."

"Then what did Darla mean by 'later'?"

"He says he doesn't remember, but she might have meant she would speak to him again before she left Morbridge."

I said, "It's all pretty circumstantial, isn't it?"

"It was until two hours ago. We got the report back from the laboratory. On the carpeted floor of the Bascombs' Land Rover, in the back, they found traces of saliva, identified by DNA as that of Darla Brown, and mixed with it were traces of sodium cyanide. Evidently these dribbled out of her mouth as her body was placed in the Rover and transported to the bog where it was buried."

"Oh, my God. Then it's true! Oliver's never been one of my favorite friends, but I suppose I rather hoped he hadn't done it!"

Neil looked somber. "The evidence is pretty conclusive. We're conferring with the Crown Prosecutor in the morning, and I expect a charge will be filed."

"I was so sure it was Derek Malone. Everything seemed to fit."

"That's why we try to be cautious about charging people until we can be sure. We've got Malone dead to rights on the robbery, and the London lads are looking for other crimes he may have been involved in."

Now I told Neil about my visit with Stella that afternoon. "You'll think I'm crazy," I added, "but I have a theory."

And I told him what it was.

Neil's ironic smile lit his face. "How very astute of you, my love. I've been thinking along those lines myself."

I was back at Bea's place the next morning when Stella came to the door, smartly dressed and looking remarkably put together.

Calmly, she said, "Your superintendent rang me up just now. They've charged Oliver."

"Oh, I'm sorry."

"No, darling. It's all right. I shan't let it happen."

"What do you mean?"

"You don't think for a moment I'd let Oliver be tried for Darla's murder?"

"But—?"

"Don't you see, darling? *I killed her myself!*"

Sitting with Neil in his flat that evening, I said, "I suppose we should be glad our guess was correct, but I feel pretty depressed. Stella was clever at deception all the way. I remember the day she drove me out to the place where Darla's body was found—how she pretended to be uncertain about finding the right road. Then, when we saw you and the other officers there, she didn't turn a hair. But yesterday, when she told me with such conviction that Oliver could never have committed the murder, I instinctively felt she was right. Oliver's too much of a wimp to go through with anything so grisly, while Stella's the type that would walk on hot coals if she thought it was necessary. But Neil, what made *you* suspect Stella?"

"It's known as experience, my dear. When you've been in this business for a good many years, you get a sense of who's lying. It's not always reliable, and I'd never try to convict anyone on it, but in this case, I felt Bascomb was telling the truth, whereas when I questioned his wife, I sensed she was holding something back.

"Once we got the evidence from their Land Rover, it had to be one or the other of them. When you so hesitantly suggested it might be Stella and not her husband, it confirmed my suspicion. Telling her he had been charged was a way of testing her reaction, and it worked."

"How did you know she wasn't lying to protect Oliver?"

"We simply told her the truth: that she would have to give convincing details of how she did it."

That story I knew, as Stella had told it to me herself.

On the fatal day, she had decided to drop in at Oliver's office when she saw Darla Brown coming out. The girl said she wanted to talk to Stella about a confidential matter. They went into a tea room and Darla told her about her pregnancy, declaring that Oliver was the father. When Darla asked for money, Stella was desperately frightened.

Darla complained of a throbbing headache, and that gave Stella the idea. She offered to take her to Herons to get money for her. Not only did Stella want to dispose of Darla as a threat to Oliver's politics, I knew she must also have felt fury at believing this girl might be carrying Oliver's child, when she herself had longed for so many years to have a child of their own.

She drove out on the moor to the road that led to the old quarry on the left and up to the Bascomb place on the right, where I had bicycled the day I visited Stella. She told Darla to wait there for a few minutes while she checked to make sure they would be alone and to give her time to assemble the money. Then Darla was to come up to the house. Stella drove on up the hill, putting the Rover in the garage, then dashed to the shed, took two prescription capsules from her purse, and filled them with sodium cyanide.

When Darla reached the house, Stella told her she had something really effective for her headache and offered her a glass of water and the capsules. The girl was dead within minutes. Stella lifted her like a child and carried her body to the Rover, drove to the bog, and dropped her in.

Filled with horror as I had been at Stella's story, I was even more appalled at her lack of remorse, at the arrogance of her final statement to me: "I knew it was risky, darling, but don't you see, I *had* to do it!"

* * *

In due course, Neil and I were able to start planning for our Paris holiday. I had no illusions that our path would be strewn entirely with roses, but the relationship at this point was satisfying to both of us. Too perfect would be suspect.

As canny Robert Browning once wrote, "What comes to perfection perishes." Sometimes it pays to listen to those Victorians.